HER
DYING
MESSAGE

ALSO BY
DONNA WELCH JONES

HER DYING MESSAGE

A Sheriff Lexie Wolfe Novel

Book 6

Donna Welch Jones

Twisted Plot Publishing

Donna Welch Jones
www.donnawelchjones.com

Printed in the United States of America

Twisted Plot Publishing

DEDICATION

To
My Fantastic Five

William C. Chapman
Sheril E. Chapman
Myrna D. Kurle
Lawrence E. Welch
Mark H. Jones

Thank you for your support and encouragement. You helped my writing dream come true!

PROLOGUE

Sheriff Lexie crept into the hospital room at midnight. The room went from shadows to brightness when she pushed the light dimmer. She leaned over the pale, unmoving woman on the bed and pressed her lips against the patient's forehead.

"Lulu, I can't find your husband's killer without your help. The murderer is getting away with Tom's death. I've done everything that I know to do, but I don't even have a person of interest. Lexie brushed tears across her cheek, then continued her plea to the white-haired woman who lay on the bed. "Most people think a stranger attacked you and Tom—was it, Lulu? Did you know the killer? Your daughter says you want to die. You can't die, Lulu. I need your help. Don't let Tom's murderer win."

Lulu's eyes labored open then immediately closed.

CHAPTER ONE

Delia swung open the office door for Lexie.

"What's up?" Lexie asked.

"A call came in that Lulu was released from the hospital."

"Is she well enough?"

Delia shuffled toward her desk. "Still not talking but moves around okay. Lulu's grandson and his wife volunteered to stay at her house."

Lexie pulled out a desk chair. "Don't they have a place of their own?"

"Bank repossessed their home in Ohio," Delia explained.

Tye's voice rose, "You're suspicious of the grandson?"

"Since I don't have a suspect, I'm suspicious of everyone, Bro. I even begged her when she was at her worse, two months ago, to help me."

Tye pulled Lexie's waist-length braid. "Begging a traumatized woman, in her eighties, reeks of desperation, Sis."

"Unfortunately, desperation sums up my current state on Lulu and Tom's case.

Delia limped toward the coffee pot. "Most of the Diffee citizens think it was a random burglary that went wrong."

Tye looked into his sister's troubled eyes. "You don't agree?"

"I don't know. Tom was brutally beaten. The attacker had a personal vendetta."

Delia speculated, "Maybe he was outraged because Tom defended his home and wife."

Lexie's features tightened. "A possibility, but I keep thinking there's evil in a fake friend or family member."

Delia fingered the clasp that held her hair bun in place. "Hard to imagine since Lulu had the biggest heart of anyone I know. Tom didn't have her personality, but he was a good guy."

"Did the doctor tell you why she's not talking?" Tye questioned.

Lexie's jaw clenched. "The killer apparently had his hands around her throat as he smashed her head into the wall. Doc said her vocal cords might have suffered damage. However, he thinks her lack of speech is a combination of brain damage and psychological trauma."

A pained expression distorted Tye's features.

"Delia," Lexie asked, "who told you Lulu went home?"

"Her daughter, Helen. She didn't want you to make an unnecessary hospital trip. She was aware that you've been there every day."

"I appreciate her giving me the heads-up."

Delia turned from her computer. "I almost forgot—Helen said it was strange how a woman who barely moved for two months struggled out of her wheelchair as soon as she arrived home. Lulu pulled fabric scraps from a drawer and arranged them into squares."

Tye's dark eyes turned to Delia. "Was Lulu a seamstress?"

"A quilter—a blue-ribbon winner at the fair most every year. When Lulu was five years old she started sewing with her granny. Helen said her mom's brain was still programed to quilt in spite of the damage."

"Weird," Tye responded.

Three pairs of eyes turned toward the front door as a rattle signaled the entrance of a petite blonde woman.

"Can I help you, Dana?"

Dana's gaze bounced from Tye to Lexie. "No way am I talking to you, Deputy. Sheriff Lexie I need to discuss something with you—alone."

Lexie opened her office door and glanced back at Tye with widened eyes as she followed Dana.

"Please sit. Dana?"

"Yes, Dana Jenkins. Your brother harassed my daughter, Starla, during that Wendy Elliot investigation. He thought my daughter killed that girl and I want nothing to do with that Cherokee asshole."

"Officers consider all possibilities. Tye's investigation of your daughter wasn't personal."

Dana's chin jutted forward. "It was personal to me."

"How can I help you?"

Dana twisted an unlit cigarette between her fingers. "Starla was raped."

Lexie's body stiffened. "Did she say who hurt her?"

"I promised I'd keep the man's name a secret."

"How can I help if you won't tell me?" Lexie heard the irritation in her own voice.

Dana's tone challenged, "You can investigate and find out on your own whether it's true."

"Do you think Starla lied?"

Dana glanced toward the window. "I don't know. My daughter isn't above lying to get what she wants."

"What's her reward for lying about rape?"

"An excuse for flunking a class and my sympathy."

Lexie tried to make visual contact, but Dana's baggy eyes diverted to the floor. "You think there's a chance Starla's telling the truth?"

"Starla was different when she came home that night. Her blouse was ripped. She cried when I asked what happened. She's a good drama queen but it seemed real. The next morning, she refused to attend school. Her neck was bruised and she walked funny."

Lexie frowned, "Did you take her to the hospital?"

"I tried. Starla screamed at me. She said she wouldn't graduate if I had a fit."

"So the alleged attacker works at the high school?"

"Yes," Dana mumbled. "I promised her I wouldn't tell. The other issue is she may be lying. I don't want to accuse an innocent man."

Lexie ground the pen point into her notepad. "There's no proof of rape and you're not giving me the suspect's name?"

"I'm no part of it if you find out for yourself."

Sarcasm rippled through Lexie's words. "It's difficult to have an investigation when there's no proof a crime was committed. I can't charge the person even if he exists."

"I do think Starla told the truth—for a change." Dana stood with her hands gripping her waist. "You must investigate because other girls are in danger." She swirled around then tromped out.

Lexie hollered Tye into her office.

He leaned against the door frame. "What's up?"

Her words were taut. "We have a rape case, or we don't."

"Is this a guessing game?"

"At this point—yes. Starla claimed a high school employee raped her. The girl has a history of lying and promiscuity. Her mother thinks she's telling the truth, but she's not sure enough to point a finger."

"What does she expect us to do without facts?"

"Dana told me to search for a criminal that may not exist. As she put it—I must protect the other girls in case there actually is a rapist."

"High expectations."

"You dealt with Starla during Wendy's case. Do you think she'd make up this story?"

Gruffness invaded Tye's tone. "I have no doubt she would. I've never met a teenager so manipulative and hateful. She slept with her boyfriend's best friend. It didn't even faze her that it would hurt the guy."

"Dana said Starla was concerned about passing a course. From her statement, I assume the alleged rapist is one of her teachers."

"If this goes public, he's fired, and Starla can claim that prejudice is why she failed."

Lexie tapped the pen. "He may have said she'd pass if she kept her mouth shut, which is likely what happened because Dana said her daughter didn't want his name divulged. Maybe Starla was so hurt and upset the day it happened that she blurted to her mother without thinking. I'll head to the high school and find out whether Principal Bradford has any insights."

"You want company?"

"No, if your wife sees you she'll ask why you're there."

"Jamie has a talent for relentless questions."

Lexie retrieved keys from her purse. "I'm sure Principal Bradford will help snoop. Either way this goes hurts the school's reputation."

CHAPTER TWO

Lexie parked her patrol car, and trotted up the steps of her alma mater. The place had deteriorated over the last eighteen years. The three-story brick structure was scarred from years of neglect. The red hue of the bricks had turned brown, and paint peeled from the window frames. The forest that backed the structure was the only thing that gave the place life.

No secretary inhabited the outer office. Lexie called across the room, "Mr. Bradford?"

"I'm here," he answered.

Lexie walked toward a small conference room.

Bradford reached out, "To what do I owe this visit, Sheriff? His large hand shook hers softly. It surprised anyone who first met Bradford that the massive man had a gentle voice and a big heart. He weighed at least 300 pounds, and was a half foot taller than Lexie's five seven

"May we sit for awhile?"

The principal ran his fingers through his white wavy hair. "Having me sit—that's worrisome. Is there a problem?"

Lexie's eyes narrowed. "I don't actually know."

Bradford leaned back. "Now I'm apprehensive and confused. As I tell the students—use your words."

"This conversation is confidential. I received an allegation that a school employee raped a female student."

Bradford's face whitened as he sunk deeper into the chair. "Who?"

"The informant didn't tell me. She wasn't sure whether or not the teen was lying, and she didn't want to ruin a man's life over a possible lie."

"Who's the girl?"

"This is confidential," Lexie reminded.

"I understand."

"Starla Jenkins."

Bradford's nostrils flared. "That girl has been a thorn in my side since she walked in the front door her freshman year. I almost fired a janitor because she made up a story about him touching her. She's verbally abusive to girls who don't meet her *pretty* criteria. I don't believe a word she says."

"The story didn't come from Starla directly. She confided in someone else—that person told me. Starla didn't want the story public."

"Trust me, she's up to no good."

"Probably, but I can't rule out rape because of her past."

Bradford sighed from deep in his chest. "I suppose you can't, but you're wasting your time. That girl has a motive for all the crap she pulls."

"I've never heard you speak negatively about a student, Mr. Bradford."

"I believed her when she said our janitor molested her. I reprimanded Gene, and would've fired him if another student hadn't come forward. Wendy saw Starla coax Gene into the storage closet, and then Wendy heard Starla immediately start screaming. The injustice I almost performed still weighs on my heart."

Lexie's tone hardened. "It's time to put that aside. If there's a rapist on your staff, Starla isn't the only girl who's in danger."

"Of course, of course—you're right. How can I help?"

"First, give me a list of Starla's teachers, and her current grade in each class. Second, a list of all the girls who are failing a course or courses that's taught by one of Starla's male teachers."

Bradford rose. "Your second request will take a while. I can get you Starla's class list right now."

He pulled a form from a file cabinet, made a copy and handed it to Lexie.

"Thanks. I won't make anything public until I come up with proof."

"I appreciate that. I'll keep an eye out for inappropriate behavior between staff and students."

"Good idea."

———— • ————

Lexie read the form as she walked toward the cruiser. Seven teachers on the list, including Ms. Crawford who'd ruled the halls of Diffee High for at least forty years. Starla was in Jamie's computer class. Lexie didn't recognize the names of three male teachers. At the end was Tye's father-in-law, Jim Evans.

She gripped the steering wheel. *Tye and Jamie's father hated each other.*

Jim will take personally any digging into his actions. Jamie will blow up if Tye confronts her father.

When the phone buzzed, it lit up Tye's name.

"I almost hung up, Sis. What took so long?"

"I wasn't ready to tell you what I know," she admitted.

"Why is that?"

"Starla is failing your father-in-law's class. Even though we know he's innocent the very investigation is likely to get him on your back."

Tye's voice cracked, "We can talk about Jim in the morning."

The connection went dead without farewell.

Surely Tye wasn't upset because his father-in-law was on the list.

CHAPTER THREE

Tye's truck grumbled as it followed the rocky road to Loretta's house—a mansion on a hilltop. It was out of place in Diffee, a small country town.

He didn't want to visit Loretta. He'd never liked the prissy blonde in high school, and she'd become even more conceited as she aged.

He knew his questions would open an old wound. He was about to dig into a trauma she'd kept hidden for over twenty years. He rang the doorbell and waited.

Loretta opened the door. Her hair was a mess of spiked gel knots. No makeup and a splash of red on a white nightgown completed her unkempt performance.

Tye assumed the dark spot on the gown was wine. Not from the glass held in her hand, but from earlier in the day as revealed by the stiffness of the stain.

She grasped the door frame. "Why are you here?"

"To discuss a case."

"I'm busy."

Tye leaned toward his former schoolmate. "Busy drinking?"

"My business—my house."

"This is official—answer my questions or I'll take you in."

She held the door open. "You're a pain in the ass."

Tye moved past her. Her odor assaulted his nose. *Perhaps it was an attempt to cover the liquor smell by mingling it with her perfume.*

The perfect living room that he wasn't allowed to even drink water in on a previous visit was strung with dirty clothes. A liquor bottle dripped onto the white sofa.

A cord hung from the wall. "Where's your stereo unit?"

"Sam took it when he destroyed my life."

"What are you talking about, Loretta?"

"My husband fooled around with a younger woman. I told him to get rid of her or get lost."

"When did he leave?"

Her words floundered. "I kicked him out two weeks ago."

"I haven't heard any town gossip."

"I've kept it quiet—embarrassed. Everyone thinks I'm perfect: my hair, my clothes, my face, and my beautiful home." She took a swig from her wine bottle. "I was the prettiest, richest woman in town. Now I'm a betrayed wife."

"I'm sorry about that, Loretta."

"I don't want your pity," she belched, "just leave me alone."

"That bottle isn't making your life better."

A mischievous grin parted her lips. "It already has—I hold the bottle close late at night. It's also a great pain deadener."

"I won't tell anyone," Tye assured her. "You let the story out when you're ready."

"Spread the word so I won't have to tell the tale of my cheating husband. All the jealous witches will gloat because he found someone else."

"Again, I'm sorry. I'm here about another matter."

Loretta gulped from the bottle. "Make it fast. My bed is calling."

"A few months ago, you told me that my father-in-law got you pregnant when you were in high school."

Her words hissed out, "You promised you'd never tell!"

"I haven't told anyone. There's an accusation floating around that one of Jim's current students was raped." Tye paused, "You can't tell anyone about this."

"I don't plan on speaking to anyone ever again."

"How did Jim seduce you? Did you approach him first?"

She banged the bottle onto the coffee table. "You think it's my fault?"

"He was a grown man and you were a teenager. It wasn't your fault. Were you attracted to him? Did you want to have sex with him?"

"Hell no! He smelled like an animal—all smoke and sweat."

"Did he force you into sex? If not, why did you?"

"I had intercourse with him so I'd pass his class. I'd have flunked my junior year if I failed his class. A big joke to everyone at the school."

"Where did you have sex?

"In his filthy hell hole office."

"Once?"

"Every week until I told him I was pregnant. He was furious because I wasn't on birth control. He arranged for the midwife that aborted my baby."

"You were never tempted to turn him in?"

"That would've been stupid. It would've negated the purpose of doing it in the first place. I'd have flunked and not graduated the next year with my friends." Her voice calmed. "Who did he hurt?"

"I can't say. The person who reported it wasn't sure if the teen was lying or not. Jim wasn't identified as the perpetrator."

"I guarantee if there was any nastiness, your father-in-law was part of it. I didn't want my baby killed. He said DNA would prove he fathered the kid, and there was no way he'd let that surface."

"I'll prove he's a perpetrator," Tye stated.

Loretta reached for her bottle. "That'll leave your marriage in the same dump as mine."

"I'll risk that possibility."

She tightened a throw pillow against her stomach. "You promised you'd never tell my story."

"You want it to remain a secret even though it substantiates the claims of his newest victim? Don't you think Jim should get what he deserves?"

"You tell and I'll deny it. Keep me out of your mess—I've got enough humiliation to deal with already."

Tye moved toward the exit.

At the door, she faced him and clutched his shoulders. "I'm so sad."

He backed away, "It'll get better over time."

"I don't think so, but maybe if I keep consuming my bottles of courage I'll forget why I'm so despondent."

Tye drove home worried that Jamie would read his mood. One negative word about her father would start a blowup.

After twenty minutes, he walked in his front door. "Where are the boys?"

"Your mom took them out for pizza."

"Not like her to invite our rascals anywhere."

Jamie spread mustard on bread slices. "She was as snippy as ever. Playing good grandma must give her ego a lift. Gabriel informed her that he had to stay home because his daddy was due."

"Seth?"

"No offense, but he was more interested in a chocolate shake than you."

"Not surprised, Seth has his priorities." Tye pulled her to his chest.

She pushed back. "Did you find a girlfriend? You smell like a perfume factory."

Tye felt sweat beads forming on his forehead. "Loretta was drenched in the stuff. Probably an attempt to cover up the liquor stench that surrounded her."

"How close did she get?"

"She gave me a semi hug."

Jamie fisted a dishrag. "I haven't seen her in the last few days. Was she in town?"

"She asked me to tell you that she and Sam split. Loretta said she kicked him out. I don't think that's the honest version of the story. She said for us to spread the word. She doesn't want to tell the tale of her desertion."

"What's the real story? He get tired of supporting a queen?"

"Sounded like he found a new woman."

Jamie grimaced, "Wow, that'd rip her guts out. She's the most self-absorbed person I've ever known."

"Sam knocked her down a few notches. Let's keep the other woman story to ourselves. It'll get out soon enough without our help. What's for supper?"

"Ham sandwiches—thought I'd take a break since the boys are gone."

"Works for me."

"Loretta's always had a crush on you. Next time, tell her to cry on the shoulder of someone else's husband."

"Glad to do it."

CHAPTER FOUR

Lexie's two-year-old, Sky, sang about people on the bus going up and down as the pair headed for Red's house at 7 o'clock.

Lexie's gut churned at the thought of her little redheaded daughter being subject to her stepmother's sharp tongue.

Red had promised he'd care for Sky. Lexie couldn't refuse him time with the daughter he adored.

She stopped the car in front of Red's house. Sky's small backpack jiggled as she ran toward the door.

Lexie opened the door and hollered. "Red, Sky's here."

"Come in," a voice snarled. "He's taking a dump."

Gina sat hunched in a recliner. Her puffy features formed into disgust. "I don't know what Red was thinking. Bringing Sky here when I feel like shit. Our baby is due in two weeks, and he puts me on babysitting detail."

"Red assured me that he'd watch Sky—not you."

Gina's glassy stare studied Lexie's face. "Well, he can't stop the racket she produces, and her stuff scattered over the living room. The little brat never listens to a word I say."

Sky clung to Lexie's leg. "Children can feel when someone doesn't like them."

"Don't get all dramatic. I never said I didn't like her. She's just too much to deal with in my present condition."

Lexie bit her tongue to keep from pointing out that Gina's attitude was just as nasty before pregnancy. "If Red has changed his mind Sky can go to day care."

"You'd like for him to get mad at me. We'll take her this Friday, Saturday, and Sunday. It'll be at least six weeks after the baby is born before Sky can visit again. My baby can't be around her germs." A smile played at Gina's lips. "Red's excited about having a baby he doesn't have to share with you."

"He's a good father."

She sang out, "My baby is a girl!"

"Congratulations."

Gina's head cocked to the side. "I won't dress my baby like you do Sky. She'll wear pretty dresses and bows in her hair. No jeans or overalls. She's a little doll not a tomboy."

Lexie bit her lower lip. "Have you decided on a name?"

"Jennifer Jane."

"That's cute."

Sky called "Daddy!" as Red trotted down the steps.

"Honey," Gina complained, "tell your child to get her shoes off the sofa."

Red's arms stretched toward Sky. "Come give Daddy a hug. How's my favorite girl?"

Sky giggled as he swirled her.

Gina whispered an aside to Lexie. "Not his favorite much longer."

Lexie's chest tightened. She longed to slap Gina across her hateful mouth. Instead she turned toward Red. "I've got to leave so I won't be late for work. Call if the visit is too much for Gina in her condition."

Her condition being an obnoxious bitch.

"I'll take care of Sky. Will you bring her over for a quick visit when the baby gets home?"

Gina's word flared out. "What?"

"I said *quick*," Red seethed. Then he turned his words back to Lexie. "I can't wait to see how Sky reacts to her baby sister."

"I'd be happy to bring her for a short visit." Lexie's eyes turned towards Gina's angry face. "I promise we won't stay over thirty minutes."

Gina's bottom lip protruded, "I'm going upstairs to rest."

Lexie gave Sky a hug and a smooch. "I'll call you before bedtime."

"I'll take good care of her, Lexie."

"I know you will."

"Bye, Mommy."

Lexie gave a final wave as she exited. "Have fun with your daddy."

Lexie chewed on her thumbnail as she drove toward her office. Her dislike for Gina was increasing to the level of Gina's hatred for her. *There should be a special punishment for people who use children as hate objects.*

Delia offered a cup of coffee as Lexie walked in the door.

"Thanks. Where's Tye?"

"He's sitting in your office. I think there's something heavy on his mind."

Lexie closed the door then sat on the edge of her desk. "What's weighing on you, Bro?"

"My father-in-law's name on the list of Starla's teachers."

Lexie sipped her coffee. "Too soon for worry—probably nothing to do with Jim. Starla has a bad reputation. Aside from that, she has three other male teachers."

Tye slowly exhaled, "I have plenty cause for worry."

"Why is that?"

"During the time I investigated Wendy's murder, I received a call from a local woman. She told me that I should investigate Jim," Tye paused.

"Because?"

"Jim molested her when she was in high school."

The words flew from Lexie's mouth. "Who was the woman?"

"I promised not to tell. She said if I ever did, she'd deny it. I interviewed her yesterday about the accusations against a school employee. She knew Jim would rape a teenager."

"Did she talk about how the relationship was initiated? Rape? Flirting?"

"He manipulated her into sex for a passing grade."

"Just like Starla's situation."

"Exactly," Tye agreed.

"Now I know who my investigation will center on," Lexie stated.

"You mean my investigation," Tye corrected.

"I meant what I said. This is too close to your home life. Jamie's a daddy's girl. Accusations against your wife's father could destroy your marriage."

"I'm the logical choice. I met the staff, and some of the kids during Wendy's murder investigation. I'll join the school faculty under the pretense of teaching a safety course. I'll blend with the staff and find the truth."

"What if you find out Jamie's father is a rapist?"

Tye's words were flat. "I arrest Jim and throw him in jail."

"Is this revenge because he forced Jamie to put your twin sons up for adoption when you two were in high school?"

A sheen of sweat glistened on Tye's forehead. "It's about him having to pay—for a change—for his evil behavior."

"I'm not assigning you this case. There's too much personal turmoil attached."

"I'm the right person. You're involved in Tom's murder case."

"Which is going nowhere; no leads, no witnesses, and no hope. I can work the high school case."

Tye shrugged, "I'll go look for jaywalkers—apparently that's all I'm good for."

"Come on Tye, you know you shouldn't investigate a case that involves your father-in-law."

"I'm the best person for this case."

Lexie shook her head no.

She heard Tye kick the back door open as he escaped the office.

Delia stood in Lexie's doorway. "Boy you pissed him off."

"I gotta do what I gotta do."

"Helen phoned while you were busy with Tye. She wants you at Lulu's house as soon as possible."

"Did she say why?"

"Lulu clutched a couple of fabric squares and screeched intermittently. Helen can't figure out what's going on."

"Call her back and tell her I'm on my way."

CHAPTER FIVE

Lexie watched as Lulu sat at her machine furiously sewing tiny fabric pieces together. "Did you want to see me?"

Lulu's eyes were rounded and wild. She pushed back from the machine, limped to a cabinet, and pulled out a pile of squares. She shoved them at Lexie's chest.

Lexie set them on the table then reached to steady the old woman.

A hoarse moan seeped from Lulu's throat. She scrunched the squares and fisted them toward Lexie a second time.

She fingered the squares. Each pattern was different, each a combination of unmatched fabrics. She moved the top square to the bottom. Lulu snatched the bottom one, and placed it back on top.

Helen raised her hands in the air. "What's going on?"

"I think your mom's giving me the clues I begged for when she was in the hospital."

Lulu nodded, then she struggled back to the machine where her frantic sewing resumed.

Lexie leaned down and kissed her cheek. "I'll return for the rest."

The elder pressed her lips together in an almost smile.

Helen walked Lexie to the squad car. "You think the quilt blocks are clues?"

"They mean something to your mom. I don't know if they'll ever mean anything to you and me. Delia belongs to the same quilting guild as your mom. I'll see if the members can help figure out what she's trying to tell us."

"Good luck," Helen said.

"I'm afraid this task requires more than luck."

CHAPTER SIX

The phone rang at 3 o'clock Saturday morning. Lexie pushed the button before the second ring. *Red's baby is probably on the way.*

Helen's voice cracked, "Mom is dead."

"I'll be right there. Don't let anyone move the body," Lexie instructed.

"Why?"

"Don't move the body," Lexie repeated.

Lexie phoned the medical examiner then got dressed. Thirty minutes later she arrived at Lulu's house.

Mike, the medical examiner, looked up as she approached the body. "No sign of foul play. Her body finally gave out from the emotional trauma of her husband's death and her injuries."

"Take another look at Lulu's body at your lab. I'll bag her dress, underwear, and bedspread and then drop them by your lab for examination."

"I'll get back with you as soon as possible, Sheriff."

Lulu's grandson, Paul, hovered near the conversation. "Something wrong Sheriff?"

"Just being thorough. Your grandmother gave me clues a few hours ago and now she's dead."

Excitement mingled with Paul's words. "She gave you clues to Grandpa's killer?"

"Yes. Did you hear anything suspicious last night?"

"Nothing, and I would've because my wife and I sleep in the bedroom next to Grandma."

"Did you find her body?"

"I heard that funny groaning noise she makes, but it sounded different than usual. I ran into the room and checked her pulse." Paul's voice wavered, "She was gone that fast."

"You console your mom while I take some samples from Lulu's bedroom."

Lexie studied the room. Lulu's body was on top of the bedspread. No turned down covers, and she hadn't changed to a nightgown. Nothing looked suspicious in the environment. Lulu would've been an easy kill, no fight in Lulu to disturb the bedroom if she was attacked. If DNA, from a murderer, were present it would be on the dress or bedspread. She took a few samples."

"Helen," she called, "come into the sewing room."

Helen joined her in the small room. Lexie visually surveyed the room.

"I left right after you did," Helen reported. "Mom still labored at her machine. I kissed her cheek, but she didn't look up. It was like she knew her time was running out."

A partial square was still under the machine needle. Lexie's eyes searched the room for the square Lulu was working on during her previous visit. Her visual search landed on a white scrap of fabric thrown in a trash can behind the door. She pulled out the wrinkled piece and flattened it on a table. *The white shape might be a house.*

Lexie held the piece in the air. "Who threw this away?"

Helen's shoulders lifted. "I guess Mom did. Perhaps it wasn't what she wanted."

Lexie set her path directly toward Paul and his wife, Mary. "Who threw away this fabric square?"

"I did," Mary readily admitted. "Lulu always kept everything neat. I didn't think she'd want something thrown on the floor."

Lexie accepted the explanation—for now. Mary probably didn't know she'd thrown away a clue.

She pulled Helen aside. "Did you tell your son and Mary that I thought the fabric squares were clues?"

Helen's hands knotted together. "I mentioned it when I was leaving, but they were watching television and didn't comment. I guess they didn't hear me."

"I'll call as soon as the medical examiner finishes examining your mother's body."

"Do you think it will take long? We need to make funeral arrangements. Do you think someone caused Mom's death?"

"It looks like natural causes as a result of her previous injuries, which of course still makes it murder. I don't think anything new happened tonight, but I must make certain. Did Lulu and Tom have money?"

"You wouldn't think so as hard as she worked at the restaurant. However, she and Dad saved almost $300,000.

"Who gets the money?"

"Fifty thousand dollars each for me and my two sisters. The other

$150,000 was willed to their six grandchildren."

"I'll get back to you about the timeline for the funeral. The medical examiner's team has transported Lulu's body to the lab."

———— • ————

Lexie dropped off the evidence at Mike's lab, and then drove toward her office. Thankful, for a change, that Sky was with Red.

Exhaustion set in, and she turned toward home instead. Hopefully, a few hours of sleep would revive her alertness and she'd resume the investigation.

Before she crawled into bed, she pushed in Tye's number. "I'll be in late—tough night."

"What happened?"

"Lulu died in the early hours of the morning. We'll go over it when I get to work in three or four hours. Oh, I forgot it's Saturday. I'll tell you Monday."

"You sound exhausted."

"If you want the high school case, it's yours."

"I do, but why did you change your mind?"

"It's necessity, not logic. Lulu's case has blown up and I've got to figure out the killer, preferably before her funeral."

"That's a short timeline. You get some rest."

Lexie crawled between her sheets. Her last thought being, *I'll regret giving Tye Starla's case!*

CHAPTER SEVEN

Monday morning Lexie dropped Sky off at day care, and then parked in front of the medical examiner's office.

"Natural causes, Mike?"

"No reason to doubt it," he grunted. "Why did you?"

"Suspicious because Lulu seemed better. I thought maybe the killer didn't want that to happen."

"The word around town is that their deaths were the result of a home invasion—robbery that went bad."

"I heard the rumors, but there's no proof. Of course, there's no proof against or for any other scenario, either," Lexie admitted.

"You want Lulu's body released to the funeral home?"

"Wait until Wednesday morning. I'm trying to figure this out before Lulu's friends and relatives arrive for the funeral."

Mike smiled. "I get it—a gathering of suspects."

"Something like that. Did you test for poison in her system?"

"Didn't know that was a concern. No discoloring on her face, no bubbling of the skin, and there were no suspicious odors when I examined her body at the house."

"I know it's a long shot, but please check it out."

"Sure, and that'll give you more time to investigate."

"That works for me."

———— ◆ ————

Delia and Tye looked up expectantly as Lexie entered the office.

"I heard about Lulu," Delia whimpered. "Breaks my heart she and

Tom met with such cruelty."

"I want your help with her case."

Delia's head jerked, "Me?"

"Yes, you and a couple of her other guild buddies. Who are the most experienced?"

"Shirley and Pam are the best seamstresses."

"I don't necessarily want the best sewers. The women who know the most pattern names and quilting history are the ones who will help."

One of Delia's fingers flailed in the air. "That'd be Roberta and Marian."

"Call them and find out if they can get here at 10 o'clock."

"They'll ask why?"

"Tell them I want help with Lulu's case. It's confidential. Ask them to bring books with quilt patterns."

A hint of excitement sang in Delia's words. "I'm on it."

Lexie motioned Tye into her office. "What's your high school plan?"

"I'll volunteer my services to Bradford. I'll offer self-defense courses—one for guys and one for girls."

"Bradford promised me a list of flunking girls and their teachers. The list should be ready today. Also, Starla's other three male teachers are Weathers in Algebra, Demetrio in Spanish, and Kasey in choir."

"I'll check them out."

"You can get to it. I hope Jim isn't the bad guy."

"That's both of us—later."

CHAPTER EIGHT

Tye followed Principal Bradford into his office. "I'll handle Starla's case. Lexie is tied up with Tom's murder."

Sadness slowed Bradford's response. "That was the most hateful act I've ever heard. Someone cruel enough to kill defenseless old folks."

"The worst," Tye agreed.

Bradford handed him a sheet of paper. "Here's the list Lexie requested. Do you have a plan?"

"With your approval—yes. I'll instruct self-defense classes in the gym. I'll show up every day for a while. Eventually, I'll blend in and not look like a suspicious visitor."

"That sounds good."

I'll collect information on Weathers, Kasey, and Demetrio to start my investigation. Does the high school do background checks on teachers?"

"We get references from prior employers, college instructors, and acquaintances of applicants."

"No background checks?"

"The school system can't afford the fees. I don't think it's fair to force applicants to fork out their own money," Bradford clarified.

"Maybe the sheriff's office can fund background checks on these three teachers."

"They'll get suspicious if they're centered out to fill out the forms," Bradford warned.

"Where are you stationing me?"

"All I have is a small office, in the basement, near your father-in-law."

"He'll hate that."

"True, but I don't care. Come with me. I'll show you the spot."

Tye followed Bradford down the steps. They made a sharp right past Jim's door to a small square office. An old wooden desk, and a chair with a stained-flowered cushion occupied the space.

"Sorry," Bradford apologized, "this is the best I have."

Jim bellowed, "What's going on, Principal?"

"Don't sneak up behind an old man. I about had a coronary."

"Why do you have a deputy stationed at the school?" Jim demanded.

"Tye's teaching self-defense classes."

"My son-in-law, who doesn't carry on a conversation with more than one person at a time, has volunteered to instruct thirty or more rowdy teenagers? Why are you really here, Wolfe?"

Tye's stance widened. "Are you feeling guilty about something, Jim? You sure are defensive."

A vein throbbed at Jim's temple. "I hate seeing your ugly face."

"It's mutual."

Jim's voice rose, "Why are you really hanging around?"

"I'm following up on rumors that a drug dealer is in your student body—keep it quiet."

"I haven't heard any talk in the teacher's lounge."

"Obviously," Tye sneered, "the informant didn't publicize his accusations."

"Stay out of my sight. It's bad enough teaching these little punks without you loitering around."

"Jim," Bradford's voice heaved, "don't call our students names."

"Sorry Principal, I forget what a softie you are. These kids play you like a fiddle."

"You're late to class. Get to work."

"Right," Jim tramped up the steps.

"I wonder how your wife turned out so well with Jim as a father," Bradford remarked.

"You and me both. I'll do background research on Starla's teachers, and plan my classes at the sheriff's office. I'll see you tomorrow."

CHAPTER NINE

Marian and Roberta arrived forty minutes before their appointed time. Marian shrilled out, "Lexie!"

Lexie flushed the toilet, "I'm coming."

Roberta was a petite woman of probably seventy-five. Marian was likely five to seven years older. Delia was the baby of the group at sixty-four.

The visitors stood on either side of Lexie—an obvious preplan. On the count of three, each gave her a cheek kiss.

"I'm not complaining, but I'd like to know what earned me this affection?"

Roberta piped, "You're going to find Lulu's killer."

Marian's words were hushed. "We know it wasn't a stranger."

"How do you know?"

"Because Helen told me she couldn't find her mama's gold cross."

Lexie filed away the fact that Helen didn't tell her about the missing jewelry. Then she asked, "Do you know anything else about the cross?"

"It was Dutchman hid. Only close family knew where to find it," Marian explained.

Lexie didn't know what "Dutchmen hid" meant, but she'd leave that question for Helen.

Lexie arranged the quilt blocks across the conference table in Lulu's order. "Ladies, I believe these quilt blocks are clues to Tom's killer. Lulu fervently worked to finish them before she died. She made sure they got to me."

"Doesn't look like Lulu's work. She was always meticulous," Roberta commented.

Marian wagged a finger in front of Roberta's face. "Good lord, woman, did you forget our friend was brain-damaged?"

Roberta's face flushed.

Marian's voice rose, "Let's get this investigating done before the bad guy gets away."

Delia joined the group at the conference table. The room fell silent as each block was scrutinized.

"That one," Delia pointed to the block retrieved from the trashcan. "I'm pretty sure is a house."

"It's a church," Roberta corrected. "That point is a steeple."

Lexie pulled it aside and wrote "church" on her notepad.

The three concentrated on a circle within a square.

"Big O," Delia exclaimed.

"I'd have gotten it, but you blurted it too fast," Marian rebuked.

Lexie shook her head. "What does that mean?"

Marian's words hurried out. "Sometimes quilters put Xs and Os for kisses."

A church and kisses—maybe Lulu's message wasn't about her murderer, but someone she loved.

"It might be the first letter of someone's name," Roberta offered.

Marian chimed in, "Or a state, like Oklahoma, Oregon, or Ohio."

Delia followed their train of thought. "Maybe Lulu was telling you that the killer was connected to one of those three states."

"Unfortunately," Lexie noted, "she's got a ton of relatives in Oklahoma."

The next square looked like a pointy dog bone in the middle of a square. "What about this one?" Lexie questioned.

"An easy one—bow tie."

Lexie jotted down Marian's response.

The shape in the third square looked like a slanted rectangle with jagged edges.

"Any thoughts, ladies?"

All three slowly shook their heads no.

Lexie pointed, "This is the last one. It was still under her machine needle. As you can see, it's not finished."

Delia held the fabric in the air. "The finished side looks like half a t shape—part of hundreds of different patterns."

Marian opened her giant pattern book. All eyes searched for a diagonal rectangle that coincided with Lulu's fourth square. Marian reached the last page.

Lexie saw the crestfallen reactions. "Keep thinking about the pattern and look in other books. You'll come up with it eventually. Call me if you think of any possibilities. I appreciate your help, and Lulu would, too. Remember your work here is confidential."

Marian challenged, "You goin' to arrest us if we blab? At my age, that'd be a great adventure."

"I know you wouldn't do anything to keep Lulu's case from being solved."

Marian labored to standing. "I've been put in my place. I'll take a guilt trip home."

Roberta patted her friend's shoulder. "You're a hoot."

Marian pointed her cane toward Lexie. "We'll keep thinkin' on it, Sheriff. These old brains require more time."

The door closed behind the pair.

"That Marian is a mess," Delia chided.

"Actually, I think she's hilarious."

Lexie pulled up a chair beside Delia's computer. "Let's review what we learned while you word process."

"A church," Delia said.

"Let's list under the word 'church' what it might stand for," Lexie instructed.

Together they listed the following ideas:

"Someone she goes to church with?"

"Someone she formerly went to church with?"

"Someone who works at the church?"

"A person she met at the church during a special occasion?"

"Second one was the O." Delia started a new section on the list.

"Love and kisses—doesn't fit with a murder investigation," Lexie concluded, and then continued. "A state where the killer lives: Oklahoma, Oregon, or Ohio."

"Could also be a city, but too many to list here," Delia decided.

Lexie added, "The first letter of the first or last name of the killer."

Delia typed the words "bow tie," and they started throwing out ideas.

"A man who wears a bow tie."

"The groom at a church wedding."

Delia clapped, "The bow tie goes along with the love and kisses square."

Lexie agreed, "A church, a bow tie, love and kisses all fit together. No one knows what that rectangle means or the partially finished block."

"Don't give up," Delia implored. "I'll do a computer search for the rectangle."

"That's a good idea. First phone Lulu's daughters and tell them to get here at 4 o'clock."

Delia picked up the phone, "I'll do it."

CHAPTER TEN

"Sis is it okay if I hold up in your office?"

"Sure. What are you working on?"

"Background checks on Starla's male teachers."

Tye shut the door behind him, but he could still hear the hum of their quilt chatter.

He scribbled out then read over his curriculum notes—they'd do. He wasn't running for teacher of the year.

His next chore was to check the backgrounds of Weathers, Kasey, and Demetrio. A time waster, he was certain, but nonetheless it was necessary to rule them out. For just a second, a happy thought sneaked into his negative attitude. *How great if Jim wasn't a rapist.*

A check of law enforcement databases yielded no arrests for any of the men. References for Weathers and Demetrio checked out as legit. Calls on Kasey resulted in four no longer in service recordings. Tye phoned the main post office in Springdale, Arkansas, to inquire about Kasey's former address.

Tye held the phone waiting for the woman's reply.

"Sorry it took so long—I checked and double-checked. There's no such address in Springdale."

"Thank you."

His brain pondered why Kasey had a fake address and nonexistent references on his application form—none of the possibilities were less than bad.

Lexie's chair swirled as he attempted to pass. "Where you running off to?"

"Back to the high school in hopes I can lift Kasey's fingerprints during his lunch hour, and get a yearbook photo. None of his background information was legit. The guy is a fake."

"Oh dear," Delia's mouth hung open.

"Keep me informed," Lexie directed.

———— ◆ ————

Tye loitered into the teacher's lounge as half a dozen teachers finished their lunches. His eyes tracked Kasey's coffee cup from hand to sink. Tye maneuvered toward the sink. He pulled the cup out with a finger stuck through the handle, and put it behind a cookie jar.

He remained in the lounge. The after-lunch bell rang. The remaining teachers scattered to their rooms. Tye dropped the cup into a paper bag.

He stopped by Bradford's office on the way out.

The secretary reached a yearbook toward him. "Principal said you asked for this."

"Yep, I did."

"Gossip is you've got some secret business going on in the high school," she nosed.

He smiled. "I'm a regular Sherlock Holmes."

CHAPTER ELEVEN

Lulu's three daughters arrived together at exactly 4 o'clock. The sisters sat at the conference table: Helen, Eula, and Bea.

"Tea?" Delia offered.

"Yes, please," Helen answered.

Eula shook her head.

Bea ignored the question. "Why are we here? We've got a million things to get done."

Lexie studied Bea's furrowed brow. "You're here to help me figure out who killed your father and mother."

"I thought you gave up," Bea sniped.

Lexie shifted in her chair. "Giving up was never part of my plan. However, the clues led me nowhere."

"And we're all sitting here wasting time," Bea croaked.

Eula cringed, "Give it a rest, Bea. You're a pain in the derriere."

Bea's scowl turned to her younger sister. "We should be planning our mother's funeral not sitting around a table sipping tea. When are you going to release her body, Sheriff?"

"Schedule the funeral for Saturday."

Eula joined Bea's argument. "A week is a long time to put off burying a body."

Helen's gaze dropped to the tabletop. "More family can attend a Saturday service."

Lexie spread the quilt squares across the conference table. "These are the clues your mother left."

Bea shook her head, "Grasping at straws, I see."

"Perhaps, but it's all I've got, so bear with me. Lulu made sure I took them with me."

"Quite a stretch of logic," Eula stated.

"Three of your mom's quilting friends studied the squares. We came up with three clues—a bow tie, an 0, and a church."

"A lost cause," Bea whined.

Lexie touched the mystery blocks. "They didn't figure out this block with the rectangle or this unfinished t. We'll talk through what each square may mean."

Helen jumped right in, "Maybe Mom attended church with the killer."

"A Christian killer—that's a stretch," Bea ridiculed.

Lexie pointed toward the door. "Feel free to leave, your attitude is a detriment to finding your parents' killer."

Her eyes clouded, "I gave up, and I won't get my hopes up again."

Lexie's tone softened, "Give me a few more days. I can't guarantee anything but we can try."

"Dad didn't attend church," Helen contributed. "A member always dropped by for Mom. She hated to drive."

Lexie scooted another square in front of the trio. "Did your mom know anyone who wore a bow tie?"

Eula responded, "Not that I can think of."

"How about a wedding where the men in the wedding party wore bow ties?"

"We're in redneck country," Bea offered. "I've never gone to a black tie wedding and I doubt Mom ever did."

"One of my theories is that the church, bow tie, and 0 go together. The O may go with X as in love and kisses. Does that bring to mind an event or person?"

The sisters shook their heads.

Lexie proceeded, "The O may mean a variety of things. Call out any way the O is significant in your family. First names? Last names? City or state of residence?

Helen and Eula looked at Bea.

Bea's fingers drummed the tabletop. "They're giving me the evil eye because my son's name is Orville."

"Anyone else you can think of with an O name?"

Eula answered, "We have two cousins who live in Ohio."

"They'd be a likely pair of killers," Bea interjected.

Helen confronted Bea, "Why do you say that?"

"Because they're white trash. They've borrowed money from everyone in the family."

Eula disagreed, "They're down on their luck, not killers."

"They've been down and begging for the last twenty years. Apparently, up isn't a direction they're willing to go."

"When did you last see these cousins?" Lexie asked.

Helen answered, "They were here for the family reunion. It was the day before Dad was killed."

"Were they still in Diffee on the day your parents were attacked?"

"Sunday was the last day I saw them, but I don't know when they actually left," Eula responded.

Bea stood abruptly, "I bet it was them."

Lexie drew in a breath. "Are you saying that most of your relatives were in town the weekend before the Monday your father died?"

Helen's shoulders slumped. "Our family loved Mom and Dad none of them would hurt my folks."

"Does the word *Dutchmen* mean anything to you three?"

The sisters looked at each other before Eula answered. "Mom hid her cross in what's called a Dutchmen wood repair. Dad made the compartment on the top of her chest of drawers."

Lexie continued, "Is her cross gone?"

"Yes," Helen replied.

Eula spoke up, "That proves it was a family member; no one else knew."

"Why would someone take the cross?"

Bea piped in, "It's been a source of arguments for years. Our family was wealthy prior to 2008 when the economy crashed. Lulu's grandmother sold everything but the cross her mother left her."

Helen continued, "It was solid gold, and the cross was formed by diamonds worth a small fortune."

Eula finished the story. "The cross was left to Lulu, the youngest child. She kept care of great-grandmother when her health failed. The other three siblings resented Lulu getting the cross, and it split her family."

Lexie concluded, "Those people weren't at your family reunion?"

"Hell no," Bea fumed. "I wouldn't invite them to anything other than a hanging—their own."

Lexie shuffled her papers. "I appreciate your answers to my questions. Phone me if you think of anything to help solve this case."

"We don't have time to figure out your job, Sheriff. We have to plan a funeral and bury our mother beside our father," Bea raved.

"Hush," Eula reprimanded.

"Don't talk that way to me," Bea crowed.

Helen's face reddened, "I'm sorry, Lexie. We'll get out of here so you can continue your work. Thank you for trying."

Bea stood with hands on hips. "You two are such ass kissers."

"Better than being an ass," Eula jibed.

"For sure," Helen agreed.

Bea hurried out the door followed by her sisters.

Delia's words rang out. "I'd hate a ride home in that car."

"That makes two of us!"

CHAPTER TWELVE

At 10 o'clock Tuesday morning, Tye was so bored with hanging around the high school that he considered a move that'd cause uproar. He wanted Starla to trap her assailant—assuming there was one. If he got Starla involved, she'd tattle to her mother. Dana would blame Lexie, and Lexie would be madder than a wet hornet.

Jamie would have Tye's head if Jim were accused. *Perhaps I'll think this through for a few more days. Put off having my ears assaulted by all the females.*

He lumbered up the steps to begin his first self-defense class. Twenty or so girls gathered in the gym. Most of them stared at small screens in their hands. Starla's eyes met his. A smirk disrupted the beauty of her face. She whispered something to the girl beside her.

"Ladies, put the phones away and spread out."

"Sidney's butt spread out in the sixth grade," Starla ridiculed.

The chin of an obese girl dropped to her chest.

A couple of girls giggled, but mostly an uncomfortable silence engulfed the room.

Tye ground his stare into Starla's smug face, "Shut up, girl."

She drew back as if slapped. "Teachers aren't allowed to trash talk students."

"Thank God I'm not your teacher." Tye's eyes changed focus. "Sidney."

"Yes," she stammered.

"You're here to learn how to deal with bullies. Don't let mouth flappers hurt you. Their cruelty means there's something wrong with them, not you."

Sidney's chin lifted, "Yes, sir."

Tye turned toward Starla. "As my grandmother used to say, if you can't say something nice don't say anything at all."

"Then I'll just leave."

He shrugged, "Good riddance."

Starla strutted out followed by three girls.

A spattering of applause erupted as they exited.

"Ladies, it's time to get some work done."

———— ◆ ————

Tye almost regretted pissing off Starla. He'd about decided to ask for her assistance. She wasn't likely to help now, but she'd gotten what she deserved.

He trusted Starla even less. Likely, the little shrew manipulated her mother with a fictitious rape accusation.

CHAPTER THIRTEEN

"Lexie," Delia called, "a fax came in about the fingerprints Tye pulled from that high school teacher."

Heat rose in Lexie's cheeks as she read the words. "Oh my God!"

Delia hobbled toward her. "What's wrong?"

"Kasey's on the FBI ten most wanted list. Scary that he's taught our kids for two years."

Delia shuddered.

Lexie pushed in Tye's number. "Come back to the office—right now." She appreciated the fact that he asked no questions.

The secretary, who answered the FBI phone, was tart. "What's the problem, Ms. Wolfe?"

"It's Sheriff Wolfe. Please connect me with an agent immediately."

"Leave a message. I'll have someone phone you *if* they deem your complaint important. I monitor calls so that agent time won't be wasted."

Lexie's words caught fire. "Here's the message. There's a murderer teaching at Diffee High School in Oklahoma. He's number seven on your most wanted list. I thought your people might want to apprehend him since it's your job." She pushed the off button.

Delia grimaced, "What's going on?"

"She refused to put me through—thinks I'm a time waster."

The cell immediately started ringing. Lexie ignored it. Two minutes later a message came up. *Sheriff Wolfe—call back.*

Then the office phone rang.

Delia's singsong words flowed out. "I monitor all her calls. Can't let you waste the Sheriff's time. I'll give her your message. Good-bye."

"You're ornery, Ms. Delia. I bet she gets what she deserves—fired."

Lexie punched in the principal's cell number. "Mr. Bradford, how

35

long do the teachers remain after school?"

"They're required to stay until 3:30 p.m. Why are you asking?"

"Can you think of an excuse to get Kacey in your office after school?"

"Is he the one who hurt Starla?"

"I don't know, but there's a warrant out. I'll arrest him after the kids are dismissed today."

"We can discuss his teacher evaluation."

"He's dangerous," Lexie warned. "Your participation is optional."

"I don't want bad guys in my school. I'm happy to help. Why are you not telling me what he's accused of?"

"You're playing a role—if you act fearful…"

"I've been faking calm for thirty-plus years."

Lexie couldn't help but laugh. "I'm pretty good at faking calm myself. See you soon."

Delia hung up the office phone for the third time. "That woman isn't giving up."

Lexie fiddled with her pen. "I think she's afraid she'll get fired. Now she's trying to cover her tracks."

Tye slammed through the door. "What's the emergency?"

"Kasey is on the top ten most wanted list."

"Damn," shot out of his mouth. "What's his crime?"

"Murder," Delia chirped.

Tye massaged his temples. "What's the plan?"

"Return to Diffee High. They're used to you hanging around. I've arranged for Bradford to have Kasey in his office at 3:30. Kids are dismissed at 3:00 so they'll be safe. Have Jim think of an excuse to cancel baseball practice and send the team home. Talk to the sponsors of other high school clubs."

"What do I tell them?"

Delia piped in, "Tell them the school is being sprayed for bugs after three o'clock."

"Tye, tell Bradford Delia's idea. I'll call Houser for back up, but he'll have to be careful. If Kasey sees any highway patrol cruisers, he'll go berserk."

Tye scratched his head. "I can join Kasey in the principal's office, and question him about the allegation that a student was molested by a teacher. It'd be great if Kasey was a murderer and the school rapist."

"I like your idea. Tell Bradford to open his office door when I knock, step out, and leave the vicinity. I'll come in and arrest Kasey."

A worried expression knitted Delia's brow. "You two shouldn't take on this guy alone."

"I'll sneak two of Houser's men into the front lobby. If Kasey runs out they'll trap him."

"He'd do a lot of damage before he escaped."

"Don't worry, Delia, we'll have guns, and I don't *think* he will."

"You don't think he will—doesn't set my mind at ease."

Tye patted Delia's back. She grabbed his hand and squeezed. "Be careful."

He holstered a gun. "I'm out of here."

CHAPTER FOURTEEN

Tye repeated Lexie's messages to Bradford then went in search of Jim. He wasn't hard to find—in the basement, as usual, puffing on a cigarette.

"Get your face out of here, Wolfe. I can't have a break without you nosing around."

"Cut the drama, Coach. Lexie told me to ask for your help or I wouldn't get near you."

Jim rolled his eyes. "Help catch an imaginary drug dealer?"

"No, to arrest a killer."

Jim snuffed out his cigarette. "One of the kids?"

"A teacher is the criminal."

"Who?"

Tye's hands flattened on Jim's desk, as he leaned toward him. "Can you keep your mouth shut?"

"I probably can this once."

"There's a warrant out for Kasey's arrest."

"I never liked the look of that guy. Hated his waxed-on smile and too red cheeks—looked like he wore rouge. You've been stalking him and not me?"

"I worked on site to confirm his identity."

"Damn—how can I help?"

"The practice field isn't a safe place for your baseball team when the arrest goes down. Bradford announced over the intercom that all after-school activities are cancelled due to an exterminator coming at 3:30. You need a different excuse since the spray wouldn't impact the boys outside."

"That's easy enough. I'll tell the guys I'm sick—of them."

"Figure out something that won't crush their self-esteem."

"I'll work on it. If I gave apologies, Tye, I might owe you one."

"That's a first."

"I didn't believe any of that shit about you looking for a drug dealer. Are you out of here after Kasey is jailed?"

"Don't rush me. The classes were my cover, but I'll finish what I started since the kids and parents expect it. For safety reasons, leave the school at 3'o'clock when the students are dismissed. Thanks for your help."

Tye took the steps two at a time. *Thanks* wasn't a word he'd ever directed toward Jim. This time he meant it. He appreciated that his father-in-law no longer believed Tye was out to get him. *Jim's guard was down. If he were the rapist he'd feel free to continue his evil, and likely make a mistake. On the other hand, if Kasey was the one who attacked Starla, it was the best scenario yet.*

Tye walked into the school lobby, and caught a glimpse of Houser in street clothes. A woman cop stood beside him in jeans and a T-shirt. They looked like parents waiting for their teenager. The pair made small talk in front of the trophy case.

He passed Lexie as she stationed herself in a storage closet outside Bradford's office.

Tye settled into a worn leather chair across from Bradford's metal desk. He held his hands out to evaluate his own steadiness—still as steel. Bradford looked as calm as Tye felt.

The bell rang, and the men heard the student racket as the kids emptied the school. Fifteen minutes later, all was quiet. It was like a sudden spring storm passed.

Bradford looked out the window. "You people are good. There's actually an exterminator's van out front."

Tye knew he hadn't called it in and doubted Lexie did. "I bet Houser from HP has three or four men in that vehicle."

"Smart man," Bradford concluded.

Tye startled as a knock sounded on the door.

"Come in," Bradford called.

"You wanted to see me, sir?"

Kasey wore khakis and a pink shirt, and had permed hair. Probably mid-twenties with Kewpie doll eyes, a shallow face, and a muscular six-foot body.

"It's Deputy Wolfe who wanted to see you," Bradford clarified.

The color drained from Kasey's face. His fingers straightened then fisted multiple times.

Tye recognized the fight or flight response and quickly spit out his words. "Thanks for your time, Mr. Kasey. A female student reported that a male teacher made sexual advances. I'm trying to get some perspective as to whether or not the girl is lying. She's got a bad reputation. Have any students offered you sexual favors for higher grades? Have you witnessed inappropriate student-teacher interactions?"

"I stay to myself. I don't pay attention to the other teachers. I don't advertise it, but let me set your mind at ease. I'm not interested in girls."

Bradford gulped, "Oh."

A rapid knock sounded. Bradford moved toward the door then stepped out. Lexie moved in with her gun pointed at Kasey's chest.

"Deputy, tell her that I didn't hurt that girl!" he exclaimed.

"I don't think Kasey is the man who raped the student."

"I agree," Lexie answered. "However, I do know that the FBI is searching for him. You have the right…"

Kasey's hands trembled above his head as he backed up.

"Stay still," Tye ordered.

Kasey's hands turned to fists as he swirled and smashed in the window glass. The rotten wood frame shattered, and the man dove out into a shower of glass fragments.

Tye ran forward, leveled his gun, and fired through the broken window. He watched Kasey struggle to his feet. The man grabbed his wounded right leg, and pulled it along as he attempted to reach the parking lot.

Houser's men surrounded Kasey as he cried for mercy.

Lexie ran toward the criminal. She snapped on the handcuffs, and read him his rights.

Energy seeped from Tye's body as he watched the drama take place outside the window. His legs felt too heavy to move from the room. All the buildup then the guy dives out the window and I shoot him. I guess I'm not as steely as I thought. And there was that other thing he was trying to avoid thinking about. Jamie's father was—again—his number-one rapist suspect.

———— ✦ ————

An ambulance pulled up as Houser conferred with Lexie.

"A couple of us can take the ambulance ride with Kasey," Houser offered.

"I appreciate it. Better if he ends up in a facility with better security than Diffee."

"The FBI phoned. They'll take over at the Tulsa hospital."

Lexie rubbed the back of her neck. "I imagine they'll get credit for our catch."

"I don't think so. A television station already asked to interview you. Quite a story when a killer led the high school choir for two years. An agent said he tried to reach you."

"Did you tell him I was busy?"

Houser grunted, "I told him to keep his ass out of the way while you finished your work."

"That was close enough. Here comes Tye. He's sure dragging his feet. Will you have one of your guys interview him? We need an accurate report of the shooting."

"We'll take care of it. Good job, Sheriff."

Lexie squeezed his shoulder. "Thanks for always being here for us."

"Three reporters are headed this way. You're caught, girl, and I'm getting in the ambulance. Good luck!"

———— ◆ ————

Lexie lost her Wednesday and Thursday workdays due to the aftermath of Kasey's arrest. Reporters hounded her, and a morning show recorded her statement. The FBI agent apologized for their clerk, who was new on the job. He tried to reprimand Lexie for not answering follow-up calls from their office. Lexie informed him that the Diffee Sheriff's Office and the Oklahoma Highway Patrol didn't require assistance. She originally phoned them because she thought it was their case. She quickly realized the case belonged to her and not the FBI. "You're welcome," was her last comment to the gruff agent who carried out the tongue lashing.

CHAPTER FIFTEEN

Lexie went from no clues to a multitude in Lulu's case. There was little time for follow-up due to Kasey's drama. Today was her last chance to put the puzzle pieces together—or maybe quilt blocks was a better description. The funeral service was at the Baptist church tomorrow, followed by a luncheon for family and friends.

She was on her way to Bea's house to interview Orville—the only O name in the family.

Bea accosted Lexie on the front porch.

"Orville said you wanted to question him. That's not necessary. My son isn't a suspect because his name starts with the wrong letter."

Lexie's response was flat. "My job is to follow all the leads."

Bea stomped her foot. "You're grasping at straws."

A man walked up behind Bea. He was around five feet three inches tall, with a slender built. He looked like a twelve-year-old boy.

Lexie doubted that anyone of Orville's size could handle Tom. He was a crusty old farmer who'd developed muscles handling livestock and plowing fields.

Orville patted Bea's shoulder. "Mom, I don't mind answering questions. I've got nothing to hide."

Bea's anger focused on Lexie. "He shouldn't be treated like a criminal."

"It's okay, Mom."

"Get it over with, Sheriff. We have important things to do and you're wasting our time."

"Orville alone," Lexie responded.

Her lip curled, and her hatred bore into Lexie's face. Lexie returned the glare.

"I never," Bea seethed.

"Walk with me, Orville," Lexie requested.

Their steps moved in unison as they circled the stone house.

"Why do you think I killed Papa and Granny?"

"Lulu left a quilt square with an O sewn on it. Since your name starts with that letter you became a person of interest."

"Logical, in a weird way."

"Did you have good relationships with your grandparents?"

"Always with Granny, but not with Papa from the time I turned twenty-one."

"Why is that?"

"I came out. Papa couldn't handle having a gay male in his family. He told me he'd always love the boy I was, but not the sissy I became."

Lexie stepped over a puddle on their path. "Were you at the family reunion?"

"No. I come from a family of old-school rednecks. None of them know how to deal with my lifestyle."

"Sounds heartbreaking—left without a family."

Orville exhaled, "It was until I met Demarco—my partner."

"Your mother cares a great deal for you."

The corners of his mouth turned up. "I thought all mothers loved their kids."

"Your father?"

"He's around, but not around me. I'm one of the reasons Mom filed for divorce. My dad told her to choose between us. She told him not to let the door hit his ass when he left."

"How does Demarco feel about all the pain your family caused you?"

"He knows some humans are too ignorant to understand that some of us are wired differently."

"Did your dad attend Tom's funeral?"

"He was there, but he hung close to the back door. When I caught up with him, on the church lawn, he spit a wad of chew into the grass at my feet."

Lexie's questions continued as they walked toward the barn. "Did he get along with your grandparents?"

"Okay, I guess. They sided with him when Mom wanted a divorce. Papa understood why Dad despised me."

"Can you think of anyone who might have reason to hurt Lulu and Tom?"

"Other than controversies over my life choice, and Granny's gold cross they got along with everyone, as far as I know."

"I heard about the cross. Was there anyone in particular who was more aggravated than the others?"

"Generally, my mother is the one angry about everything. Since the cross ended up with Lulu, it's likely Mom will inherit since she's the oldest daughter. Lulu's oldest sister, Nell, is the one who threw a wild-ass fit. The brothers stayed out of the fight for the most part."

"For the most part?" Lexie repeated.

"Uncle Clive, through his wife, voiced the opinion that he's the oldest sibling thus the cross should follow his line. Aunt Nell and Uncle Clive did nothing to help my great-grandmother when she had Alzheimer's— only Granny. Their additional argument was that Granny and Papa were well off, and didn't financially need the cross."

Lexie turned their meandering back toward the front yard. "Your aunt and uncle wanted to sell the cross?"

"That's what it sounded like to me."

Lexie pulled the front gate open. "Thanks for your input, Orville. I appreciate your time."

She rubbed her forehead as she approached the cruiser. Once inside she continued to massage her head. Her hand searched for aspirin in her purse, but once she found the bottle it proved to be empty.

Lexie steered the car away from Bea's house and toward Lulu's place. There, she'd question Paul, the homeless grandson, who'd ended up with Lulu's roof over his head.

Her thoughts caught on the diamond and gold cross controversy. Maybe the church quilt block was meant to represent the cross. Or the half t on the unfinished block might be the cross. Or I may be way off!

When Lexie arrived at her destination no one responded to her knock. She pulled the screen door open and hollered "Hello?"—no answer.

She circled the house. The F word resonated from a shed in the back.

The squeal of rusty door hinges announced her arrival. "There's some colorful language radiating out your door."

The grandson rose from a dilapidated mower. "Sorry, Aunt Bea ordered me to mow the lawn before relatives started showing up for Granny's funeral. She didn't bother to mention how to get this piece of crap running."

"I'm here to ask you a few questions."

"You think I killed Granny and Papa so I'd have a place to live?"

"The rumors beat me here. Their deaths have turned into an opportunity for you."

His face reddened. "An opportunity for you and a few relatives to sling shit. I'm having a hard time, but I'm a decent guy."

"Do you know anyone who had reason to hurt your grandparents?"

"Papa was grumpy at times, but he was a stand-up guy. Granny was as close to a saint as anyone I've ever known. I don't know who'd want to hurt them. Didn't a stranger attack them?"

"Perhaps, but I investigate all possibilities. Where were you the Monday night they were attacked?"

"That bar on the East end of town—Clyde's Southern Comfort. I was with Ted James. We bonded after we were fired on the same day."

"Anyone in your family wear a bow tie?"

"Not that I've ever seen. We don't wear ties either."

"Thanks for your time, Paul. I'm sorry for your loss."

Lexie heard the mower-cussing resume as she walked away.

When she got to the car, she sat behind the wheel and pushed in numbers.

"Hey, Clyde, this is Sheriff Wolfe. Do you happen to remember if Paul, Lulu's grandson, was in your bar last Monday?"

"Generally, I wouldn't remember, but I do because I kicked him and Ted out when they started a ruckus."

"What kind of ruckus was that?"

"Ted got tired of Paul mooching beer money."

"What time did you give them the boot?"

"Close to midnight," he answered.

"Thanks."

Maybe the pair doubled up to steal cash from the elderly couple.

CHAPTER SIXTEEN

Lexie settled into her work chair as Tye strode toward her.

"Why are you here after-hours, Sis?"

"Red agreed to take Sky tonight, and tomorrow morning so I can work Lulu's case. Gina's probably chewing him out as we speak."

"How's your case going?"

Tye sat on the corner of her desk. "Nowhere. The more I'm around Starla, the less I think a school employee molested her. She's one mean girl. Then there's Jim; he snarls every time he sees me. He keeps asking why I'm not gone."

Lexie yawned, "That's nothing new."

"What about Lulu's case?"

"I'd like Lulu and Tom's murders solved by one o'clock tomorrow."

"Why the deadline?"

"After the service and the lunch, my suspects will scatter here, there, and yonder."

Tye scooted from her desktop. "Who are you looking at?"

"Paul, a grandson, now resides in their home, so he benefited. The daughters and all the grandchildren are in the will—substantial amounts. That same grandson is broke. Their deaths resulted in a windfall for him. Bea's son, Orville, caused a family upheaval when he came out. Story is that Tom was bent out of shape because his grandson was gay. Maybe Orville or his partner, Demarco, came back to defend Orville's honor."

Tye settled into a chair. "Could a woman have done it?"

"A female, or Orville for that matter, would unlikely have the physical strength to beat Tom to a pulp."

"In that case," Tye asked, "why haven't you ruled Orville out?"

"Because his name starts with an O. His partner has an O at the end of his name."

Tye's expression went blank. "I'm sure that all makes sense to you, but I don't know what you're talking about."

"Sorry, I forgot you were out of the loop."

"Get me back in," Tye urged.

"Lulu lived long enough to sew quilt squares. She shoved them at my chest the last time I saw her. I concluded that the blocks were clues to Tom's killer. Delia and a couple of quilting ladies came in to help me decipher Lulu's clues."

Tye stood, "Let me have a look at them."

"No offense, but your experience with quilts consists of sleeping under them."

"I'd still like to see the blocks."

Lexie spread the squares across her desk. "According to the guild ladies, this one is a church, this is a bow tie and this is an O. They didn't recognize the fourth pattern. The fifth one was half finished, but it looks like a t."

"So that's where the O for Orville and Demarco came from?"

"Yes. However, it could also be the first letter of the killer's state or city of residence. At first we discussed X and O as in kisses, a church wedding, and a bow tie worn with a tuxedo."

"Not likely to see a bow tie in Diffee."

"True, and family members said no one in their family has ever worn a bow tie."

Tye picked up the bow tie block. "I'll expect an apology shortly or better still—a raise."

Lexie rubbed the back of her neck. "For what?"

Tye's chest puffed, "I know what the killer drives."

"Are you magical, or is it ESP?"

"A bow tie is the Chevy logo."

Lexie squealed, "You're brilliant! I'd never have thought of that."

Tye bowed, "Thank you very much."

Lexie speculated. "Lulu picked a red, gray, and black striped swatch of fabric for the bow tie shape. I bet the vehicle is one of those three colors."

"I bet you're right."

"Mr. Smart Guy do you have any idea what this rectangle with the jagged edges represents?"

"Not a clue! I'm headed home before Jamie throws out my supper. I'll arrive at the church at 8:30 in the morning. I assume I'm supposed to match Chevys with owners."

Lexie fist bumped his shoulder, "Exactly."

CHAPTER SEVENTEEN

The church gathering room was filled with Lulu's family, friends, and, with some luck a murderer.

Lexie heard the clatter of dishes as church volunteers picked up empty plates and utensils. Most of the people listened or told stories about Lulu during the luncheon. Peals of laughter erupted when Bea's estranged husband, Junior, told how Lulu stomped her feet, and pounded his chest when he accidently dropped her sugar bowl. Her kitchen floor was covered with fragments of glistening sugar and glass.

Hot breath carried Lexie's name into her right ear.

Roberta's hand shook as she pulled Lexie into an alcove between the gathering room and kitchen.

Roberta's words hastened out. "I know what the fourth pattern is."

She delivered the pattern name into Lexie's right ear.

Lexie's finger touched her own lips. She squeezed Roberta's hand, "Thank you."

When Lexie re-entered the room she noted a couple saying their good-byes. They soon found out that no one was leaving until she had the killer in cuffs.

She shouted above the combined conversations. "Attention everyone, it's time to find Tom and Lulu's killer."

The voices hushed, and the church doors closed almost in unison. A law enforcement officer stood in front of every exit—six total.

"What's going on?" A man shouted from the second table. "I got farm work this afternoon."

Her response was low pitched and steady. "We're playing *Find a Killer.* I'm thinking this won't take long. Lulu told me who killed Tom, but I have gaps in my information."

"I heard she couldn't speak," a neighbor spouted.

"She left me messages nonetheless."

"But she couldn't write," another spoke up.

Lexie's body stiffened, "I know the killer drove her to church in a Chevy."

The rumpling complaints ended.

"I know the killer's name likely has an 0 in it. Orville and Demarco come stand beside me. You both have 0 in your names so you are persons of interest. Also, I was informed that Demarco has a black Chevy parked in the back lot."

Demarco stood in front of the group. His arm wrapped around the smaller man's shoulder. "I've never taken Orville's granny to church."

"Did Orville ever take her to church in your car?"

The bigger man stood silent.

Lexie waited.

Demarco hesitated then confessed, "Probably two or three times."

She stepped closer to the pair. "Perhaps Lulu tried to identify Demarco through hints about Orville. Sound plausible?"

Demarco's words strained. "Doesn't make any sense that I'd kill people that I didn't even know."

"Out of love for your partner—Orville."

A buzz rose from the crowd. Apparently, Orville wasn't completely out—he was now.

Lexie beckoned Paul, "Come join my game."

Paul's feet drug as he moved forward.

"An O in your name, Paul?"

"No ma'am."

Did you live in Ohio?"

"Yes, ma'am," he confirmed.

"Did you ever take your granny to church?"

"Many times."

"Story around town is that you killed your grandparents to get their house."

"Full-of-shit gossip."

Lexie's jaw set. "Why is that, Paul?"

His eyes surveyed the crowd. "Now that they're dead, the house belongs to their three daughters. I didn't gain a home—I lost one when they died."

"Look at me, Paul," Lexie ordered. "How about that cash you'll inherit from their will?"

His eyes widened, "I've never heard that."

Lexie challenged, "You didn't know the grandchildren will inherit?"

Bea's agitated tone rose from beside the buffet table. "The grandkids weren't told about the money. Mom called it a special gift—a surprise—not to be divulged until after she and Dad died."

Lexie's accusatory words shot toward her. "Perhaps Paul went through their papers. After all, he resided in their home."

Helen's finger shook at Lexie. "You have no right to sling accusations at my son. This is illegal."

"No one is making anyone answer questions." Lexie's head tilted. "I do admit a person looks suspicious if he won't cooperate, though."

Lexie beckoned Junior, "Come join us in the front."

Clots of dirt dropped from his dirty boots as he walked forward. He stopped within a foot of Lexie. "Two fine people are dead, Sheriff, and you're making a game of it. Perhaps we didn't elect the right person."

"You're right about two good people dying. However, you don't seem interested in finding the killer. Is that because you're the murderer?"

His words came out with a spray of spit. "I didn't kill anyone. You're fishin' to find someone to lay this on."

"Did you ever drive Lulu to church in that shiny red Avalanche of yours?"

"I drove my mother-in-law to church; that makes me a good man, not a killer."

"Why did you kill them, Junior? Perhaps I should use your given name—Orville."

"Nobody calls me Orville. That was my father's name," he snarled. "I'm leavin'—you got nothin' on me."

"I think you understand by now, Orville Junior, that I've got you in a noose. The more you wiggle, the tighter it becomes."

A soup pot cascaded toward Junior's head. His hand flung it aside, but celery, carrots, and potatoes clung to his shirt soaked in soup stock. He whipped around to face the aggressor. "What the hell?"

Bea shuffled forward, and then beat the soup spatula against his head. "You son-of-a-bitch—I know why you killed my folks."

The room fell silent. Lexie gave her head a toss to dislodge vegetable pieces from her hair. "Why did he kill them, Bea?"

"He wanted them dead before our divorce was final so he'd have the legal right to half my inheritance. Another month and he'd have no claim."

A couple of carrot chunks rolled off Junior's shoulder as he dried his head with a dishtowel. "Tough luck, witchy wife. They're dead, and we're married. Everything you get is half mine."

Lexie pulled out her gun. "Unfortunately for you, Junior, you'll get zero. I'm arresting you on two counts of first-degree murder. Lulu left a message about the killer. The person who broke her sugar bowl committed the crime."

Junior made a beeline toward the exit. He called back, "Sheriff, you can cram that stupid sugar bowl story up your ass."

Lexie pointed her gun as she walked forward. "When you told this room full of people that you broke her sugar bowl, you admitted that you killed Tom and Lulu."

Lexie read his rights, and then she and Tye secured him in the back seat of the squad car.

Tye followed her out of Junior's hearing range. "Is this case going to hold?"

"Quilt squares probably won't standup in court. Fortunately, a hundred people heard his tirade about getting the inheritance money. Of course, his lawyer will have a fit when he finds out my frivolous evidence. I'll get a court order to search his apartment and vehicle. When we find the cross, he hasn't got a prayer of going free."

"How did you know about the sugar bowl?"

"The quilt pattern we couldn't figure out was named *The Broken Sugar Bowl*. It's a rectangular shape with jagged ends. Roberta frantically told me about the pattern after Junior conveyed his funny story about breaking Lulu's sugar bowl."

"You're telling me that you didn't know, before the service, that Junior was the killer? Pure luck that he told the sugar bowl story?"

"That sums it up."

CHAPTER EIGHTEEN

Tye felt the Monday morning blues as he lumbered down the steps to his desk in the high school basement. He knew he shouldn't have pissed off Starla. She was his only link to the rapist—molester monster—Jim. Now Tye's chances of making Jim pay for all his wrongdoing was little and none.

He startled as he recognized the visitor who sat on his designated chair.

"Starla?"

"Deputy?"

"What are you doing here?"

Starla leaned toward him. "Even more interesting is what you're still doing here, Deputy."

"I'm teaching the self-defense course you took for five minutes."

She fluffed her hair. "Nice cover, but I doubt it. Why are you really here?"

"Do you not watch the news?"

"I heard that story, but before that, I was told you were searching for a drug dealer."

Tye's eyebrows pinched together. "From Jim? He's the only person I told."

She gnawed at her bottom lip. "He didn't believe your story nor do I."

"Pillow talk?"

Her body slumped.

"I'm here to help, Starla."

Her voice choked with emotion. "Why would you? My own mother didn't believe me."

"Actually, she did believe you; that's why I'm here. Are you ready to go public with your accusations against him?"

"Everyone thinks I'm a slut. Jim is a popular coach—respected. They'll say it's revenge because I'm failing his class."

Tye studied her face. "I know another girl he raped."

Her eyes widened, "Who?"

"You know I can't give out that information."

Anger clouded her eyes. "Why didn't she turn him in?"

"She was a coward. Didn't consider that she'd be saving other girls—like you—from the monster."

A creak at the top of the stairs sent a wave of panic through Tye.

"Starla, I'll crouch behind my desk. Move toward Jim's office like you were looking for him."

Tye curled his long frame to the floor.

Jim's gruff words carried easily to his ears. "Starla, what are you doing down here? I told you Tye's nosing around. He could show up any second. Get out!"

Tye heard the bitch tone mingle in Starla's words. "Coach, I'm thinking a C isn't enough reward for what you took from me."

"You pass—that's our agreement."

"I require a B to bring up my overall average. You know it'd look good on my college applications."

Rapid-fire words exploded from Jim's mouth. "You little whore. Yell rape and here you stand negotiating for more. You'd have to make me real happy to get a B. None of that crying and whining shit."

"It was my first rape—not sure of the correct etiquette."

Jim's harsh laugh ground into Tye's head. "You're a spirited girl."

"Tell me when and where?"

"I'll get back to you. Get out of here before Tye shows up."

Tye's muscles ached from the squatted position. No way could he get out without being seen. He flexed his arms and waited. He heard Jim make room reservations for Thursday night. There was no way to know which motel he picked.

Principal Bradford's voice carried from the top of the stairs. "Tye?"

He felt Bradford's presence in his small office.

"Have you seen Tye this morning?"

"No, and I hope I don't," Jim grumbled.

Tye raised his head above the desk surface and shook it no.

Bradford nodded. "Coach, why aren't you upstairs monitoring the halls?"

"That was last week."

"You didn't show up last week so you're on duty this week."

"Shit, I'll get there in a few."

"You'll go now," Bradford dictated. "I'll follow you up."

"I don't need an escort."

"Had me fooled."

Tye listened to the footfalls on the staircase before he uncurled and stretched his body. He hurried to Jim's desk. The phone book lay open, and an ink mark circled the words River City Cabins.

A smile played at Tye's lips and a quiet "Thank you, Jim" seethed out. He jogged up the steps then paused at the door to make sure the coast was clear. He slipped into the hall.

Tye raised his chin as Bradford acknowledged his presence. He followed the principal to an empty classroom.

"Thanks, I was caught for sure without your quick thinking."

Bradford pulled at his chin. "Why were you hiding behind the desk?"

"I was listening to a conversation between Starla and Jim."

"And?"

"Coach arranged a meeting to raise her grade to a B."

Bradford gripped a chair back. "This is the devil's work. I'll fire him right now."

"It's too soon. We must catch him in the cabin with Starla. Without proof, it's his word against hers, and she'd lose that contest. Keep this between us, and you'll have enough proof in a few days to axe him."

"It's in your hands. I've never dealt with a pervert in all my years in education. I hate to think about how many young women he's molested."

Tye thought it best not to comment.

"You keep Starla safe."

"I will, sir. I have a self-defense class with the boys in thirty minutes after that I'll consult with Lexie. I'll give you the heads-up when we have proof."

"You know where to find me."

Tye moved toward his basement office. A puff of smoke blew toward his face as he passed Jim's door.

"Aren't you supposed to monitor the halls this morning?" Tye's gut wrenched. *I wasn't supposed to know that.* His next words scrambled out. "Working on lesson plans or figuring out how to have a winning ball team would also be good uses for taxpayer's money."

"Stay out of my face, asshole. Why are you still around? You got Kasey."

"My last self-defense class is today."

"Finally, good news."

Tye snatched notes from his desk and tromped up the steps. *Jim didn't respond to my monitoring statement; maybe he didn't catch my blunder."*

———— ◆ ————

"Where's Lexie?" Tye asked when he returned to the office.

Delia stopped word processing. "Sky's ear started hurting at day care. Lexie took her to the doctor then home. You look like something is heavy on your mind. She said to phone if anything came up."

"Nah, it'll keep until tomorrow."

CHAPTER NINETEEN

Lexie woke when Sky whimpered beside her. She rested her hand on Sky's forehead—cool. She made her way to the kitchen. A bowl of cereal quieted the stomach growls from missing supper the night before.

The ringing of her cell quickly propelled her toward the device before it woke Sky. "Hello?"

Silence met her greeting. "Who is this?"

"Red—I'm on the hospital phone."

"Is the baby here?"

"Yes," croaked from his throat.

Chill bumps erupted on her arms. "What's wrong, Red?"

His words cracked, "My baby has Down syndrome."

Lexie's chest ached as seconds passed. She didn't know the right words.

Red hesitated, "I'm sorry to bother you, but..."

"You're not bothering me. Your words left me speechless."

"I know that feeling."

"How is Gina?"

His words rumbled out, "Distraught, angry, humiliated to name a few of the many things she's screamed."

"Is the baby—Jennifer—is her heart okay? I read that about half the babies with Down syndrome have heart defects."

"The doctors are running a series of tests. Already did the karyotype to confirm the diagnosis. Gina said she wasn't using the name Jennifer because that's her favorite name."

"Give Gina some time. I know this is a major shock—not her little dream girl."

Anger seeped into his words. "She told me to name the baby. She didn't

56

care what I named *it*."

"What name are you using?"

"Haven't thought about names."

"I almost gave Sky the name Hope. What do you think of that?"

"Seems appropriate since I'm going to require a lot of it."

"Think about it."

"Don't worry about bringing Sky over when the baby comes home. It's not the happy occasion I imagined."

"Then we'll make it happy. Sky is excited to meet her sister. I bought her a baby doll to teach her gentleness. She calls the dolly sissy. Every once in a while, she checks the diaper and says 'poopy' then holds her nose."

Red laughed, "That's our girl."

"Sky's excited to see her sister."

"You're right; I'll call you the day she comes home."

Lexie's tone softened, "Please phone with updates. I'll worry."

"I will. Tell people about her diagnosis. I'd rather not see or hear the shock if I tell them myself."

"Hang in there," Lexie said.

"I'll try—life has a way of screwing me."

Lexie didn't reply before the phone went dead. She was thankful for the reprieve.

She studied the ceiling. Her thoughts didn't form into words or actions that might help Gina and Red accept their newborn daughter. *It was like envisioning a perfect little girl, and having their child not fit that mold. It'll take time for them to find a new dream for their tiny girl.*

CHAPTER TWENTY

"Hey Sis, how's Sky?" Tye's words shot across the office as Lexie entered.

"She's great. We caught the ear infection before it got too bad. She cried when I mentioned staying home from day care. It's party day for the kids born in May."

"She's such a party girl. Good luck when she's sixteen."

"I'll probably need it. Where's Delia?"

"She and Sloan are taking a day trip to Eureka Springs."

"I forgot," Lexie admitted

"I have news on Starla's case."

"Well, tell your tale, Bro."

Tye went through the happenings from the day before. He finished with, "I still have a crick in my back from being wadded under a desk."

"It's a miracle you weren't caught."

"Maybe I was caught," he confessed,

Lexie sat back, "What?"

"I screwed up when I mentioned that Jim wasn't monitoring the hall—he was actually scheduled the week before."

"He didn't react?"

"No, he was too busy preparing his next insult."

Lexie fingered her phone messages. "Hopefully, it went over his head. Talk to Dana about Starla's involvement in the setup for Jim. She may refuse Starla's participation in the drama."

"I'll take off in a few minutes to tell her. First, let's talk through a plan."

"We'll record the call when he phones and gives her final details. The recording will prove his intent."

Tye paced, "I thought we'd stake the place out and catch him naked in bed. Starla can lock herself in the bathroom. We'll catch him in a compromising situation with a student."

"We can't risk getting Starla injured. Anyway, it looks like entrapment."

Tye kicked the desk, "Damn."

"Starla can call from our office to receive his directions. If he phones sooner, she'll have to put him off. She'll tell Jim someone is with her. She can arrange to call him back then come directly to our office so we can record."

Tye's expression tightened. "Is a recording legal?"

"One-party-consent calls are legal. The recording shows intent, which points a finger at Jim. It's not a matter of what he deserves; it's what we can prove."

"Unfortunately," Tye jeered.

Lexie's face became solemn. "Red phoned me early this morning."

"The baby arrived?"

"Yes. She has Down syndrome. He struggled when he told me. He's upset and I imagine Gina is in shock. Call him."

"Sis, I don't know what to say."

"He's your best friend—think of something."

"I'll visit Dana and find out if she'll let Starla participate in the undoing of Jim."

"As the mother of a daughter, I probably wouldn't."

———— ◆ ————

Tye pulled out his cell phone when he got behind the wheel. He punched in the number and hoped Red wouldn't answer, but he did.

"I hear you got a new girl?" Tye said.

Red's words seemed distant, "I do."

"Another little redhead?"

"Her hair is the same color as Sky's."

"Is she healthy?" Tye asked.

"Doc's running tests."

"How are you holding up?"

Red's tone was tense, "I don't know what to do with a 'special' baby."

"I've seen you with Sky. You're a good father. That's all your new little one requires."

Red's tone relaxed, "I guess I can handle that."

"I know you can," Tye confirmed. "What's her name?"

"Lexie suggested, and I agree that Hope is the right name for my new daughter."

"Sounds good. I'm looking forward to tickling her toes. Call me when she gets home."

"Won't take her long to remember you."

"Damn straight. I'm on a deputy mission; I'd better get busy. Phone if you need anything."

"Tye?"

"Yes."

"Thanks for calling."

"You're welcome. Later." *Lexie was right. I'm glad I called Red.*

CHAPTER TWENTY-ONE

A burly guy sat on Dana's front porch smoking a cigarette.

"I'm Deputy Tye Wolfe."

"Don't harass me. I've served my time. It was self-defense, not murder," he argued.

"I'm here to see Dana. Who are you?"

The man flicked ashes into the weeds beside the step. "Gil Jenkins."

"Is Dana around?"

"Yep, she's inside sulking 'cause I pissed her off."

"I've been known to piss off a woman or two."

"It's easy to do with Dana."

"Good luck with that," Tye knocked on the door.

Gil stood and stomped his cigarette butt. "It'll take more than luck. Come on in. Maybe she'll talk to you."

Tye followed him into the living room.

"Hey, Dana," Gil called.

"Go to hell," she hollered from a back room.

"Want me to take Deputy Wolfe with me? He wants to see you."

Dana appeared in the doorway. "You can go to hell alone."

"I cheated on her once eighteen years ago, Deputy, and she still won't forgive me. I didn't care anything about the little tramp I screwed. I just wanted a good time."

"I was nine months pregnant and miserable, and you cheated on me."

"That's why I found her. You were big as a barn and couldn't roll over. That whore meant nothing. Deputy, don't you think a guy should get a break?"

"I stay out of personal problems. Dana, I'm here to discuss Starla's problem. Is it okay if Gil listens to our conversation?"

"If he was a good father, his daughter could've got some love from him instead of all the other males she tempts and teases."

"I didn't hang around because you made it mighty clear that you hated me."

"I never kept you from her. You suck as a father—moved off then ended up in prison for ten years."

"Not this again," he snapped.

Tye raised a hand. "I don't have time for this. Does he stay or go?"

"He can stay. Good for him to hear what I've dealt with alone."

"You expressed concern to Lexie that a high school teacher molested Starla."

Gil's arms flailed, "Someone hurt my girl?"

"Yes, someone hurt the daughter you hadn't seen in sixteen years."

"Woman, they don't let prisoners leave jail cells for home visitation."

Tye raised his hand in warning for the second time.

Dana's angry eyes focused on Tye. "That was a confidential conversation with Sheriff Lexie. None of your business."

"You knew she'd inform me. I'm her deputy."

"You think Starla lied?"

"I think she was attacked by one of her teachers."

Tye noted Gil's knuckles turning white as he gripped the table edge.

Dana's voice trembled, "Have you arrested the vulture?"

"There's no evidence. Without my input or permission, Starla arranged to meet him. I can stop her plan, and he'll go free. With your consent, she can help us get a recording and we'll have proof."

Gil's fist punched the air. "That bastard will pay."

"You get involved, and you'll earn a short trip back to jail," Tye warned.

Dana spoke slowly, "Starla says and does what she wants. If it's her plan she'll carry it out with or without my approval. She's always been a little hellion. I don't know where I went wrong."

"Maybe took after her dad," Gil offered.

Tye looked Dana in the eyes. "I'm aware that Starla is strong-willed and hateful at times. Recently I learned that her cunning and manipulation is positive under the right circumstances. It's a matter of channeling her intelligence to the right path. She figured out how to trap the perpetrator on her own. You should also know that if her plan works she'll save other girls from the pervert."

Gil probed, "Why don't you say the pervert's name?"

"I don't want your temper messing up the arrest."

"When and where is this happening? She's my daughter. I have a right to know."

"Specifics aren't set. Regardless, I don't want a loose cannon around. Both of you stay out of this."

"Shit," was Gil's last word before scrambling out the door.

Dana's lips twisted in disgust as she watched him exit, "How soon?"

"Within the week."

Dana's eyes filled with tears. "Will you keep her safe?"

"She won't be at the scene. He'll just think that she's meeting him."

"I trust you."

"I'll tell you when it's over. If Starla gives you specifics, don't tell Gil. By the way, he was an asshole to cheat on you, pregnant or not."

Her lips stretched into a smile. "Thanks."

I don't remember ever seeing the woman smile. Perhaps the result of having a life where nothing is easy.

He phoned Starla's cell and told her about the recording. She agreed to drop by the sheriff's office the next afternoon.

CHAPTER TWENTY-TWO

Tye glanced at his watch for the fifth time. Only 3:15—another hour and forty-five minutes on duty. His cell phone interrupted the monotonous traffic surveillance.

"Deputy, it's Starla."

"Has Jim contacted you?"

"It's too late for a recording," she spouted.

Tye's tone sharpened, "Why?"

"He saw me in the school parking lot after class. He ordered me to follow his truck."

Starla's voice sounded confident, but he noted a slight quiver. "Right now?"

"Yes. I'm in the lot waiting for him to pull out. I told him I'd planned on seeing him Thursday. He said he'd changed my plans."

"Did he say where you're going?"

"No," she muttered. Her single word was almost lost in the motor sounds of vehicles leaving the school.

Tye swept the sweat off his forehead with a sleeve. "It's too risky. We don't know where he's taking you. Don't follow him—go home."

Two words vehemently erupted into Tye's ear. "Hell no! This is my only chance to get him. I'm not stopping. The jerk will pay."

"I'll phone the cabin office and find out if he's registered, then call you right back. Meanwhile, I'm headed toward the high school. I'll try to intercept and get behind your car."

"Okay," Starla responded then hung up.

A woman's whiny voice answered the cabin business phone.

"This is an emergency," Tye informed. "Put the owner on the line."

"Boss is out fishing," she answered.

Tye could barely hear over the television racket on her end. He shouted words into the phone. "This is Deputy Tye Wolfe. I believe that an unlawful act will take place in a cabin today. Tell me your new check-ins."

"I can't."

Tye's voice raged, "I'll arrest you for interfering with official business."

"Boss said he'd fire me if I gave out customer information."

"He won't be thrown in jail—you will. I can mark your family for surveillance in a six-county radius. I hope you have law abiding relatives."

She spilled the information, "Only two check-ins scheduled today."

"Names?"

"Don Cox and Charlie Meacham are the two."

"Have they both arrived?"

"The Meacham guy said he'd pay cash when he got here. Cox used a credit card."

Meacham must be Jim, Tye assumed. "What's the cabin number assigned to Meacham?"

"Number 12—it's the furthest unit south."

The call ended, and Tye's brain labored the prospect of Jim knowing something was up. It wasn't probable, but it was possible that Jim figured out this was a trap. Was he leading Starla to a different location to rape her?

Tye's tone was heavy with apprehension when he reconnected with Starla. "Where are you now?"

"Coach turned right out of the parking lot and is driving west."

"I'm ordering you to turn around and go home."

"I told you—no way. We're going toward the lake. You'll catch up."

"When you arrive at the cabin, lock yourself in the bathroom. Stay on line while I radio Lexie."

"Lexie, Jim cornered Starla in the school parking lot and ordered her to follow him."

Panic formed in Lexie's belly. "Tell her to stop."

"I have—twice. She said there's no way the jerk gets away with molesting her. I called the cabins. Clerk said he was assigned number 12. It's the furthest unit South after you turn off highway 10."

"I'm on my way," Lexie snatched car keys and ran out the door.

Tye's brain jumped from one bad scenario to another. If Jim caught the blunder about the hall monitoring, he knew that Tye was in the basement when Bradford arrived and before. Tye didn't think Jim was smart enough to figure it out, but he'd also not pegged his father-in-law as a rapist. If Coach knew this was a trap, surely he wouldn't risk meeting Starla. Maybe the pervert wouldn't give up sex with the girl. Jim changed the day and likely the location thinking he'd avoid getting caught.

Tye drove as fast as possible along the curving, two-lane highway. Starla's car was nowhere in sight. He should've told her to drive slowly, but now he couldn't. The wooded areas shut off cell reception.

He maneuvered the turns that passed cabins scattered over the next few miles. The number 12 hung from the porch of a dilapidated cabin.

He parked the cruiser behind a stretch of trees then jogged forward then around the cabin. One firm push, and the back door sprang open. The place was a discarded furniture dump. Guilt welled in his chest as he remembered his promise to keep her safe. He had no idea where Jim led Starla.

He slid behind the steering wheel then sped toward the cabin office. He hit the brake as he saw Lexie's vehicle headed toward him.

"What's wrong?" She yelled through her open window.

"They aren't in 12. I'll question the clerk."

"I'll turn around and follow you."

The clerk's skin shade paled as Tye ran forward. "You told me Meacham was assigned cabin 12. Looks like it hasn't been occupied for years."

Lexie entered as the woman muttered. "I can't give out that information. You might want to hurt Meacham. I wasn't about to help you."

Lexie responded, "A young woman is in trouble. We had information she was brought here. Which cabin is Meacham really in?"

"I don't want to get fired," she blubbered.

Tye blasted, "You'd rather a young woman got hurt?"

"I don't mean no harm," she sniffed.

Objects on the counter vibrated as Tye's fist slammed the surface. "Tell us where he went?"

"Tell my boss you forced me."

"If you don't tell me the cabin number right now, I'll strangle you," Tye heaved.

The girl stepped back; her arms formed an X across her chest.

"I won't let him hurt you. Surely you've heard of me. I'm the county sheriff."

"I moved to Diffee a month ago. My name is Daisy."

"That explains why you're unsure, but he may kill a girl because you're uncooperative. Give us the cabin number right now."

Daisy's words scrambled out, "Number 6—closest cabin to the bridge."

"Get in my car, Tye. Too much activity if two vehicles pull up. I'll take the front door; you cover the back."

"He didn't figure us out," Tye said when they reached the cabin. "Both their vehicles are parked in front, which means he didn't try to hide."

"Only good news we've had today. Get in position—Jim may run out the back when I go in the front door.

Tye stationed himself beside the porch steps.

Lexie turned the front door knob—it opened. She stood in the open doorway and called out "JIM!"

"GET THE HELL OUT OF HERE!" blasted from a side room.

Lexie swung open the bedroom door. "I received a report that a criminal act was in process. Where is she?"

"What are you talking about?" he said too loudly.

"Come out," Lexie hollered.

Starla opened the bathroom door. Tears left streaks of mascara on her face.

Lexie squeezed her hand, "Are you okay?"

Her voice squeaked, "I didn't think you'd find me."

Tye ran into the room, "Did he hurt you?"

Her words were barely audible, "I'm okay."

Sweat dropped from Jim's forehead. "You son-of-a-bitch. Why are you tracking me? Get your nose out of my life." He walked toward Starla. "You filthy little wench. I'll have you expelled."

Tye stepped between them. "This isn't Starla's doing. I was in the basement when you made plans to meet her. I'm the one who trapped a rat."

Jim fumbled with shirt buttons as he spoke. "She propositioned me. She's eighteen—an adult. I'm no fool. I'd never have sex with an underage girl."

"She's your student," Lexie stated.

"That has nothing to do with you or your chump brother."

Tye pulled the handcuffs from his belt loop.

Lexie shook her head no. "A lawyer will claim entrapment."

Starla screeched, "You're going to let him get away with hurting me?"

"My hands are tied. You didn't follow directions."

Her frantic words cried out, "I couldn't. There was no time. He's not going to jail? He'll ruin my life."

"I'm sorry. I can't arrest him. I'll report his behavior to the school superintendent. He'll determine the appropriate action."

Jim's fist punched the air. "Wait until I tell my daughter how you trapped me—wanted me thrown in jail."

Tye snarled, "There's no explanation for a teacher having a student alone in a cabin."

"I came here to fish. The little slut followed me."

Lexie jabbed a finger toward his face. "Why was your shirt off?"

His lip curled, "It's hot down by the lake. Starla said she had to pee, so I walked her up here to use the bathroom. I'm a nice guy."

Starla sprang forward. Her fists attacked his chest.

Tye grabbed her shoulders and pulled her back.

An evil grin stretched Jim's lips. "Poor baby got caught playing her nasty game, and now she's having a tantrum."

Tye loosened his grasp and Starla ran out the door. Her car engine's roar momentarily broke the cabin silence.

"Well, Sheriff, since there are no charges, I'll go home to supper. Tye, this should convince my daughter you're a pile of shit." He saluted, "You two have a good evening."

After Jim left—Tye kicked the door frame. "We can't do anything?"

"The recording would've shown intent. Without it we have nothing that stands up in court."

CHAPTER TWENTY-THREE

Tye approached his dark house at twilight. Jamie sat on the front porch swing. A suitcase leaned against a post.

"Where are the boys?"

"At your mom's house. I told her you'd pick them up."

His words squeezed out, "What's the suitcase for?"

"Me—I'm leaving you. I heard how you trapped my father. You know Starla is a horny little brat, and you used her to get back at Dad. I never thought you were the kind of man who could hate anyone that much. He's a couple of years away from retirement. If they fire him, my parents will have nothing but Social Security to live on."

"I proved that your father is a rapist. I caught him in an isolated cabin with a student."

Her nostrils flared, "The only thing you proved is that you're a spiteful, vengeful man. You had that girl follow him then walked in and arrested him—entrapment. What hurts more than anything is that you didn't love me more than you hated him."

"Starla isn't the first student your father manipulated for sex. It's no telling how many girls he attacked in the past."

Jamie smirked, "Oh, that mystery woman you claim Dad molested, but you refused to supply a name?"

"Confidential."

"Funny how everything becomes 'confidential' when you have shit to hide."

His voice lowered, "The boys love you."

"On school days I'll pick them up, and drop them off at the sheriff's office at 5 o'clock."

"How am I supposed to explain your absence?"

"How about 'Daddy is an asshole and Mommy can't put up with it anymore'?"

"That sounds crude," Tye huffed.

"But it's clear and true."

Tye's heart beat as if trying to escape his chest. "Your father was always more important than me. He can give away our twins and molest teenage girls, and he's still your hero—I give up. Leave until you get your head on straight. You'll change your mind when you discover the truth about your dear daddy."

"You can apologize on your knees when you figure out you victimized my father."

"Your old man is a monster, not a victim."

Jamie pushed from the swing. "I'll get the rest of my stuff when you're at work. I won't listen to any more of your lies."

She tripped as her foot missed the bottom step. The case popped open, and clothes scattered. She struggled to standing then rubbed her leg.

Tye suppressed the urge to rush to her aid. He entered the house. Through the window, he saw her cram belongings into the case then limp toward her car.

He wandered around the too quiet house as anger boiled in his gut. Now on top of everything else, Jim had damaged, if not destroyed, his marriage. He longed to beat the crap out of him. Maybe one fist to Jim's face would diminish the fury in his body.

His cell rang out its tune. "I'm headed out the door, Mom, be there in a few minutes."

"These boys are too much for me. Jamie knew I didn't feel well but she insisted on leaving them."

"I'll be there soon."

Tye trotted to his truck. *Jamie getting Margo involved in their mess was another jab from the Daddy lover.*

———◆———

Margo tapped her foot. "Finally, you're here. I'm about to have a stroke. They've argued for the last two hours. Gabriel whacked Seth on the derriere. Seth caught hold of him then they rolled all over the floor like wild animals."

"Sorry, Mom, I'll get them out of your hair."

Margo's chin rose, "Sounds like Jamie wants all three of you out of her hair. She has some nerve, after you married down, to take off and leave the boys with me."

Tye's shoulders drooped, "Sorry, Mom."

"Believe me I'll never let Jamie pull that trick again," she blasted.

"Get your backpacks, sons, and let's get gone."

"Before we break Grandmother's heart?" Gabriel questioned.

"Is that what she told you?"

"Yes," Seth chided. "Gabriel broke her heart."

Gabriel defended, "You were the one who broke Grandma's heart. You threw her fancy pillows at me."

"Grandmother's standing so her heart isn't broken. Let's get out of here before we cause more trouble."

Margo groaned as she sank into a chair.

"Thanks, Mom. Sorry for the drama."

Margo closed her eyes as the three exited.

Tye enclosed both boys in the passenger seat belt.

"Have you guys eaten?"

Gabriel's features squeezed, "Grandma gave us yucky soup."

Seth added, "It tasted like rotten meat with burned onions."

"We'll buy fried chicken on the way home. Your mama won't be there."

Gabriel's words were matter-of-fact, "She was really mad."

"That's why she left."

"I didn't do anything wrong," Seth explained.

"No, you didn't. She's upset with me, not you boys."

"Tell her you're sorry," Gabriel recommended.

"Not that easy."

"You're not sorry?" Seth questioned.

"No, I'm not sorry. She can come home when she's ready. Right now she can cool down. She'll pick you up after school everyday, and drop you off at my office. You'll get to see your mom."

Gabriel yawned, "I'm tired, Daddy. It's been a hard day."

Tye couldn't help but smile. "That's for sure. We'll get our supper and go home."

CHAPTER TWENTY-FOUR

After a sleepless night and a hurried breakfast, Tye dropped the boys off at school.

A text from Bradford requested an update on the Jim and Starla drama—sooner not later.

The usual teens stood by the door as Tye entered the high school. One looked at him with more distain than usual. Bradford's secretary signaled Tye to enter his office.

Jim sat in a chair opposite the principal. His back was straight, fists clenched, and his face expressed pure hate. A rolled newspaper sprang from his hand and smacked Tye on the face.

Tye shook his head, "Grow up."

Bradford ignored Jim's juvenile behavior. "Tye, have you seen the morning paper?"

"No—busy with my boys."

"Look," Bradford directed.

Tye retrieved the paper at his feet and read the headline, *Coach Accused of Molesting Student.*

Jim's words growled out. "You've ruined my reputation, asshole."

"Tone it down," Bradford warned.

Tye eyed the paper. "I know nothing about the article."

"We're not fools. We didn't forget your son works at the newspaper," Jim ranted.

"He worked for the paper; now he's at college. Another indication of how much you suck as a grandparent. I don't know how the reporter got the information. It wasn't from the sheriff's office. We don't advertise things that make us look bad."

Jim's eyes protruded, "Then that little slut did it. I'll have her ass."

Bradford's expression darkened, "Who are you calling a slut?"

"Starla, of course—she set up the trap with my soon-to-be ex-son-in-law."

Bradford's fingers tapped the desk surface. "Go home. You're on leave with pay while our school attorney sorts out your mess. Calling Starla a slut and threatening to get her ass won't help your case."

"I'm not going anywhere but my first class," Jim taunted.

Tye pulled his gun. "Go of your own accord, or become an Internet star when the students photograph you leaving the building with my gun drawn behind your back. Photos last forever."

"You'd shoot an unarmed man?"

"That'd be my preference, but I'll humiliate you instead."

Jim turned as he reached the door. "I can use a few days off. Nothing can diminish my happiness now that Jamie dumped you. Daddy knows best."

"She'll eventually figure out her father is a pervert."

———— ◆ ————

Tye found Starla sitting on her front step. "Why aren't you at school?"

"You think I'm going face to face with Jim?"

"I escorted him out of the school a half-hour ago. There'll be an investigation to determine his fate."

Her top lip curled, "So he may be back in a week or two?"

"I don't know, but I doubt it. He was in a secluded location with a student. I think the school system can hang him even though law enforcement can't."

"I may have to change schools my senior year or be home-schooled?"

Tye's tone hardened, "I told you to drive home. Without the recording, we have nothing that proves intent."

"Now that Coach's actions are public, he can't snake away. Dad said we'd get him one way or another. The newspaper article asked other girls he hurt to come forward. Who knows, maybe it won't be his word against the school slut," Starla reasoned.

"Gil contacted the paper?"

"Mom told him to butt out—he didn't listen."

"Don't go anywhere near Jim."

"Oh, I won't. Daddy told me to wait and see where the scum ends up."

"Your mom and dad here?"

"Mom's at work. I don't know where Dad is."

"Call if you need help," Tye instructed.

"Yeah right, that really worked yesterday," Starla disappeared into the house.

Tye drove the cruiser toward the highway. He'd park in a shadowed area and catch speeders until his shift ended. Contribute a little money to the city coffer. That's what his usefulness boiled down to. He'd failed Starla, angered Jamie, and Jim went free instead of occupying a jail cell.

CHAPTER TWENTY-FIVE

Five minutes until 5 o'clock and Lexie's cell phone rang. She wanted to ignore it but one glance at the caller's name and she pushed the button.

"Any news on your baby, Red?"

"That's why I'm calling. Gina's mom was at the hospital so she offered to bring them home. They'll arrive in about thirty minutes."

"Seems like a quick release. I guess that means the baby's okay?"

"Surprised me, too. I thought you'd want to drop by after you pick up Sky."

"We'll come, but just for ten or fifteen minutes. I don't want to stress Gina. See you soon."

Dread formed in Lexie's chest. Gina's hatred would make this a difficult visit.

———◆———

Lexie heard the screaming as she unlatched Sky from the car seat. The breeze picked up the sound and riffed it through the trees.

When the pair reached the porch, Lexie heard Red's voice boom from inside. "How could you?"

Lexie hated bringing her little daughter into the argument, but she'd promised Red and told Sky she'd get to see her baby sissy. With a little luck, their entry would interrupt the fight.

Lexie knocked, and Gina's mom opened the door.

"Not a good time," she warned.

Red's voice sounded from behind his mother-in-law. "Come in, Lexie."

"Keep her out of my house," Gina screeched. "Look at her gloating face. She's a monster."

His voice choked with emotion, "You're the monster, Gina. You gave away my baby. Left her at the hospital."

"The social worker said they'd find a family to adopt her. She's not alone. Volunteers rock and feed the babies who don't have families."

Red's facial muscles quivered. "My daughter has a family."

"She isn't my baby," Gina yelled.

"Well, she's mine," Red boomed.

"I gave up custody."

Red's hands flexed into fists, "You can't give away my custody."

"I won't look at her everyday knowing she'll never be okay," Gina grimaced, "We'll have another baby—a normal baby. It's her or me."

"Go home with your mother. I'll drop your stuff off in a few days."

Gina gasped, "YOU MEAN—"

"I don't want you around my baby. I'll go undo your mess. Don't be here when I get home. If you are, I'll carry you out."

Sky's little face scrunched as she reached for her shaking Daddy. He bent down and picked her up. She touched his face as if to sooth him.

"It's okay, honey. Daddy is sorry he frightened you."

"Sissy?"

"She didn't come home today. I'll visit Hope at the hospital. I'll tell her she has a big sister who can't wait to see her."

Gina's words stormed out, "You can't bring her here. I forbid it."

His voice calmed. "I meant it when I said for you to get out while I'm at the hospital."

Red moved toward the door holding Sky and Lexie followed.

An object plowed into the back of Lexie's head. She bent forward in pain. The book slid down her back and hit the floor.

"What the hell?" Red snapped.

"Sheriff Witch ruined my life."

"Please, let's go," Lexie begged.

The impact of the hard-covered book activated a painful throb in her head.

"Are you okay?" Red asked when they reached the car.

"We had to get Sky away from her."

"I know—our only option. Sorry you got caught up in my disaster."

"Her dream was destroyed," Lexie sympathized. "I don't blame her for throwing things."

"You're too kind. It took me a few months, but I figured out what Gina is, and it isn't good."

Red kissed Sky's cheek.

"I'll inform the hospital of Gina's betrayal and check on Hope."

Lexie bent down to fasten Sky's seatbelt. "Call when you know something."

———— ✦ ————

Ten p.m. and still no call from Red. Lexie pushed his number into her phone.

"How is Hope?"

"She's doing pretty well. Gina's mom signed my name on the paperwork that gave Hope up for adoption."

"Are you going to take legal action against her?"

"I'll use it to get rid of Gina. If she doesn't get out of my house and give me a divorce, I'll file charges against her mother."

"You're sure it was her mother who signed your name?"

"It wasn't Gina's writing," Red answered.

"Did you get Hope's release date?"

"Inpatient a few more days, because she's having feeding problems. They're trying different bottle nipples. I'll receive training."

"May I attend with you?"

"I appreciate the offer, but I can handle it."

"I know, but I need to learn what to do when Hope is visiting or you're at work."

"That makes sense."

"You sound exhausted, Red. Try to get some sleep. Phone if you want to talk. Goodnight."

"Night."

Lexie had the urge to cry, but she suppressed it out of respect for those who really had something to cry about.

CHAPTER TWENTY-SIX

Tye pressed the cell phone against his ear. "What do you want, Loretta?" His free arm held a shaking little boy whose mom plowed into a street light pole.

"Jamie was supposed to arrive two hours ago. She hasn't showed. Do you know where she is? She could've at least called to cancel."

Irritation nagged at his chest. "We're separated—remember? I don't keep up with Jamie's social calendar." Tye clicked the phone off without farewell.

He turned his attention back to the five-year-old. "Don't cry, Shawn. Your mom is going to be okay. The ambulance will drive you two to the hospital and check you out. Was she talking on her cell phone?"

"She was yelling at Daddy."

"Your dad was contacted, and he'll meet you at the hospital. Do you hurt?"

The child held up a bloody arm.

"That's a nasty cut. We'll ask the ambulance attendant to take a look."

Tye attempted to hand the boy to a medic, but the child grasped his shoulders.

"It's time for bravery, Shawn. Talk to your mom so she'll know you're okay."

"I will," he said meekly then loosened his grip on Tye.

———— • ————

Delia turned as Tye entered the office. "Anyone hurt at the accident?"

"A child had minor injuries. His mom is in worse shape, but she'll recover. Apparently, arguments on cell phones are life-threatening."

"The elementary school secretary called. She said Jamie hasn't picked up the boys. Asked me if Jamie intended to leave them until closing time. She reminded me that last pick up is 5:30."

"That's strange. Loretta called me earlier, and said Jamie didn't show up for their luncheon date."

Delia palmed her phone. "What should I tell the school?"

"Tell them I'll get the boys between 5:00 and 5:30."

He punched in Jamie's cell number—no answer. He hesitated then pressed in Jim's number.

The sound of Tye's voice activated Jim's temper. "What the hell are you calling for? Still screwing my life? You got another gut punch?"

"Cut the drama. Jamie missed a couple of appointments today. Have you seen her?"

"Don't worry about my girl. She can take care of herself," he snarled.

"She never misses the boy's pick up time. When did you last see her?"

The phone went dead. The vein at Tye's temple heaved.

Delia's head jerked, "Tye?"

"Jim's from the bottom layer of humanity."

Tye looked at the name on his incoming call. "It's Jamie's mother, Opal."

Opal's words squeezed out quietly. "Jamie left around noon for a luncheon date with Loretta. I haven't heard from her since. She promised to drive me to my hair appointment this afternoon, but she didn't come home. Do you think she's hurt?"

"I don't know, Opal. Have you called Loretta?"

"No," she answered.

"If you hear from Jamie, call me. I'll do the same."

Tye heard Jim yelling in the background. "What are you doing, woman? You better not give that demon information."

Opal's voice called back. "I'm talking to a friend. Leave me be."

Tye called the next number on his mental list. "Mr. Bradford, we're having difficulty locating Jamie. Why wasn't she at work today?"

"She took a personal day with my blessing. Frankly, she's having a tough time. Some of the parents made her the scapegoat for her father's evil. Others are mad because her husband—you—trashed their beloved coach's reputation."

"Thanks for the information."

Delia wheeled her chair toward his desk. "Do you want me to get the boys?"

"I'll do it. Hopefully, I'll meet up with Jamie. She probably decided to pick them up at closing and didn't inform the staff."

"Phone so I'll know she's okay."

"Will do."

CHAPTER TWENTY-SEVEN

Lexie jogged into the office for a quick good-bye before picking up Sky at day care.

"How was the class?" Delia asked.

"I learned a lot. Red was great. He asked questions and requested extra practice with the feeding. I knew he was a good man, but he exceeded my high regard."

The phone interrupted their conversation. "Diffee Sheriff's Department," Delia's waving hand summoned Lexie. "Calm down, Loretta."

Lexie ran to the phone, "Yes?"

Loretta cried out, "I found Jamie beside the road!"

"Is she okay?"

"She's gone."

Lexie's heartbeat escalated, "Gone?"

"She's dead," Loretta moaned.

Lexie's words sprang out, "Jamie is dead?"

"How many times do I have to say it? She's dead."

Lexie's hand pressed her chest as she made eye contact with Delia. "Did you phone an ambulance?"

"I said she's dead," Loretta yelped.

"I'll be right there. Don't touch anything." Lexie gave her order then hung up.

Delia gasped, "Tye was looking for Jamie. She didn't pick up the boys after school."

"She's dead."

Delia's tears broke free, "That can't be true."

Lexie placed her hand under the older woman's chin. "Look at me. Call for an ambulance then the highway patrol."

"What will you tell Tye?" Delia whimpered.

"I don't know. Loretta has turned into a drunk; maybe she's mistaken."

"We hope."

"Will you get Sky from day care?"

Delia nodded.

———◆———

The steering wheel was slick with sweat. She'd felt this profound sorrow only three times before in her life—after the deaths of her father and Abbey. The third event was the kidnapping of Sky. The theory Loretta was mistaken was a delusion. The tone of her voice conveyed a horror that was real not liquor induced.

If she didn't inform Tye immediately, he'd be furious. *But how do you tell your brother the worse news of his life?* She pushed in his number.

"What's up, Sis?"

Her tone was firm. "Drop the boys off at Mom's house and meet me at Loretta's place."

"Is this about Jamie?"

"Yes, Loretta found her. An ambulance was called."

Panic invaded his tone, "Is she sick?"

"Meet me at Loretta's."

Lexie pushed her hand against her chest in a futile attempt to slow her heartbeat. *I can't tell him over the phone. Maybe Loretta is wrong.*

Lexie saw Jamie's car as she drove up the hill. The driver's door stood open. She parked behind the vehicle and walked forward. Jamie's body lay face down in the rocky heap that bordered the road.

Her scream echoed, "JAMIE!"

She rolled the body over and checked for a pulse—none. She pulled the bloody blouse front apart revealing a star-shaped entry. The wound indicated that the killer shot at close range.

Lexie studied Jamie's beautiful face and kissed her forehead, "Good-bye, sister."

The siren noise got closer. The ambulance arrived first.

"Too late guys. My sister-in-law is dead. The medical examiner will take care of the follow-up—you may go."

One guy called back as he reached the ambulance, "Sorry for your loss."

She lifted her hand in response.

Houser of the highway patrol walked toward her.

"Sheriff, why are you touching the body?"

"I checked her vital signs. She's my sister-in-law."

"Dear God. Sorry, girl, but you've got to move out and let us do our job." He reached down a hand and pulled her up.

"Lexie," Tye called as he walked forward.

A patrolman blocked his way, "Stay back."

Tye flat-handed the officer's chest, "Like hell I will." His eyes caught on his wife's lifeless body on the dirt and rocks. "Jamie," heaved from his lips as he stumbled toward her.

A highway patrolman on either side of him grabbed an arm as he lurched forward against their strength. "Let me hold her," he begged.

"No," Houser ordered. "You can't touch her. The husband is always the first suspect in a wife's death. Stay away from the evidence if you didn't kill her."

Tye's face wrenched, "You think I killed Jamie?"

"Of course not," Houser growled, "but I don't want it to look like you did."

Tye sat on the dirt in sight of the body. He stared at the lifeless form. *The girl I've loved since high school. The woman I've had many harsh words with over the last few days is gone forever.*

Lexie grasped his shoulder.

"If I'd listened when Loretta told me Jamie didn't show up for lunch, she'd be alive."

"No," Houser corrected. "If she lived at all after the shooting, it was only for a short time. No way could she survive that bullet. Medical help wouldn't have made a difference."

Houser's partner came forward. "Do you think she caught a stray bullet from someone hunting in the woods?"

"No, the killer was close. A stray bullet is a good newspaper angle. If the killer thinks that we think it was an accident, he may get confident and sloppy. We'll tell the reporter, when he shows up, that we're investigating the possibility."

"Jamie stepped out of the car for some reason," Lexie observed. "It was no accident. She was shot straight on. The killer signaled her to stop."

Houser pointed out three men. "You guys check a 200-yard radius around the body. Look for broken foliage, shell casings—anything the killer may have dropped."

"Is it a suicide, sir?"

"Nothing says suicide at this scene," Houser barked.

The men dispersed, and Houser turned to Tye. "You said someone named Loretta called this in? Where is she?"

"Probably at home. That's her house on the hilltop. She and Jamie were friends since high school."

"You two come with me to interview her."

Tye turned back toward the body, "No."

Houser's drill sergeant voice erupted. "The medical examiner has arrived so you'll stay out of his way. We've got a murderer to find so get your ass up. All you can do for your wife is help us get the guy who killed her. You'll have plenty of time to mourn."

Tye lumbered from the ground. Lexie pressed a hand on his back to guide him to Houser's vehicle.

Houser questioned, "Tye, anyone bothering Jamie lately? Has she complained about problems?"

"Jamie left me. She moved out, took her dad's side when he was accused of raping a student. She thought I trapped her old man."

The trio continued the drive in silence.

Loretta sat on the front porch, a liquor bottle gripped firmly in her right hand.

Bloodshot eyes, highlighted by dark circles, bore into Tye's face. "I told you I was worried, but you didn't listen. I found her myself—dead."

"How did you find her?" Lexie asked.

Loretta took a drink. "I decided to drive into town without her. I saw her car as I drove down the hill. Then I got out, and there she was—dead."

"You touched Jamie's body?" Houser questioned.

"I got back in my car and phoned Lexie."

Lexie continued, "Then you went back to your house?"

"I was afraid."

Lexie prompted, "Afraid of what, Loretta?"

"Fearful the killer hid in the woods. Do you think I'm a bad person for leaving her alone?"

"Smart that you realized the killer might still be around," Houser consoled.

Lexie visually checked her brother. Tye stood like a pale zombie, listening—or not—to Loretta's words.

Lexie resumed the questions. "Did you see anyone on your hill today—hunters, workmen, anyone? Did you hear a shot?"

"We don't allow hunters on our land. Inside the house I seldom notice any sounds from outside. I didn't see anyone around today."

"Why was Jamie coming here?" Tye heaved.

"You're blaming me because I invited her to lunch?"

Lexie intervened, "Of course not. Someone knew she was coming or they followed her. Make a list of anyone you told. I'll get the list later."

Loretta's gaze rested on Tye's face. "I'm sorry. I know you're in shock. Forgive me?"

"Nothing to forgive—nothing matters now."

———◆———

Back at the crime scene, Houser directed Lexie. "I'll take care of the site investigation. Drive your brother back into town. I'll have an officer return his vehicle to your office."

Lexie hissed into his ear, "So you can look for evidence?"

"Let me do my job, which, hopefully, includes taking your brother out of the equation."

Lexie acquiesced, "Of course—sorry."

"Your job is to inform and interview her family. Find out who knew Jamie's luncheon plans. The killer didn't follow her. He was waiting in the clearing to beckon her out to kill."

———◆———

The siblings descended the hill in silence. Occasionally, a guttural breath escaped from Tye's lips. His only words came out as they parked at the office. "It was hard enough to tell my boys their mom left for a while. Now I have to explain she'll never come home again. How do I tell them?"

Lexie breathed deeply, "Tell them she died—the truth."

"This is their second murdered mother. How will they ever heal?"

"Your sons love you, and as long as they have their father, they'll pull through."

"I can't help them if I can't save myself."

Lexie's voice strained, "You have no choice. You adopted your boys, and you can't desert them."

Tye's words choked out, "How about my pain?"

"They need their father regardless of how much you hurt."

His head dropped.

"Get the boys in my Jeep. I'll take the patrol car since I have official business to handle."

She slid from the seat, and Tye took her place without comment.

Perhaps I was too abrupt, but Seth and Gabriel need him more now than ever. He doesn't have the luxury of sinking into a pit of despair.

CHAPTER TWENTY-EIGHT

"Mom, it's Lexie."

"Where's your brother?"

"He'll be there soon."

"These boys are running me ragged. I told Tye the other day that they were too much for me. Now I've ended up with them again. Jamie is neglecting her motherly duties. I'll have a few straight words with her. Not picking up her boys and disrupting my personal time. There's no excuse for her bad behavior."

"Mom, Jamie couldn't pick up the boys. She died today."

Margo squealed, "Oh my God! How? When?"

"Late morning."

Margo assumed, "Heart attack?"

"She was shot in the chest—murdered."

"Who killed her?"

"Investigation has just started. I called because Tye's on the way to your house to get the boys. Please be understanding. He's in a bad place."

"I don't require your behavior prompt."

"This is a heads-up so he won't have to explain why he's desolate. You've never liked Jamie. A reminder not to speak daggers about a dead woman to the widower seemed appropriate."

"They were separated—marriage failed. I'll admit I was glad."

Lexie suppressed the urge to scream. "That's the kind of crap you shouldn't say. Also, don't tell Seth and Gabriel about their mother's death. Tye will tell them in his own time in his own way."

"Anymore instructions?" Margo snapped.

"I think that's enough for now. Please be kind."

"The things I put up with. You were a bossy little thing from age four and you've gotten worse with age."

"I'll phone you when funeral arrangements are finalized."

Lexie decided to stop by Principal Bradford's house first. An easy visit compared to the sorrow produced when Jim and Opal learned their daughter was dead.

The principal and his wife, Clare, sat on their porch swing.

"Sheriff, is there something wrong at the high school?" Bradford asked.

"Not with the physical structure."

Clare responded for him, "But?"

"One of your staff members died earlier today. I thought you'd need time to prepare for the emotional repercussions from students and staff."

Clare's word erupted, "Who?"

Lexie's eyes couldn't hold the tears. "My sister-in-law, Jamie."

Bradford stood and squeezed Lexie's hand. "I'm so sorry my dear girl."

Tears flowed down her cheeks. She bit her lip. "I'm having trouble holding myself together."

"Of course you are, dear," Clare held the door open. "Come inside and sit with us."

Clare fluffed the rocker pillow before she motioned Lexie to sit.

Lexie forced her mind away from sorrow to the case.

"How did she die?" Bradford asked.

"Based on the initial investigation it was murder."

Bradford rose from his recliner, and walked nervously into the attached dining room and back. His facial muscles fought to keep his emotions in check.

Lexie focused on his eyes. "Do you know anyone who despised Jamie enough to kill her? Was there a staff member she didn't get along with or a student who failed and wanted payback?"

"Jamie has a good reputation. She tutored teens during lunch or after school if they were failing. She covered for teachers who weren't up to their lunch or hall duties. Nobody is perfect, and I'm sure there are people who disliked her. No one at my school had a killing hate for her." Bradford's expression darkened.

"What is it, principal?"

"Jamie was getting negative feedback from all her father's evil doing. Parents verbally attacked her because it was safer than confronting Jim."

"You're saying that it's possible Jamie was killed in retribution for Jim's actions?"

"You know Gary King's daughter, Megan? She's failing Jim's class. Gary got into Jamie's face. He threatened Jim through her. He was afraid Jim hurt his child."

Lexie pushed on, "Who else?"

"Gil Jenkins, Starla's dad, showed up out of the blue yelling about not keeping his daughter safe and threatened to sue the school system. He was self-righteous about his girl and said they deserved money for her pain and suffering. Dana phoned me later and apologized. She said Gil showed back up in Starla's life after sixteen years."

Lexie stood, "I've got another stop. I dropped by because I knew you'd want to schedule grief counseling for students and staff."

"I appreciate you. I'm sorry for your loss."

Clare caught Lexie in a hug as she exited.

Lexie reached the cruiser before the sobs escaped her mouth. Spent, she rested her head on the steering wheel as she worked for emotional control. Finally, she straightened her back and turned the key in the ignition. *I've got to hold myself together.*

It was less than a ten-minute drive too Jim and Opal's small wooden house. Light from the television screen flashed through the window as she knocked.

Jim hollered, "Get the door, Opal, I'm busy."

Lexie pounded. The guy was three or four yards from the door and wouldn't move his ass—called his wife instead.

Strands of gray hair caught in Opal's forehead sweat. "Not expecting anyone. Sorry I look a mess."

"May I come in?"

"Of course, sometimes I forget my manners."

Jim turned up the television volume. "You hens go cluck somewhere else. I'm watching my show."

Lexie pushed the television off button. "I have something important to say."

"It can wait fifteen minutes until my show is over. I've had enough of the Wolfe siblings sticking their noses in my life. Come to think of it—get out of my house. Can't stand to look at you."

"Jim," Opal reprimanded.

"Don't Jim me. Anyone with the same DNA as Tye isn't welcome in my house. Turn my show back on, woman."

Opal's tone was apprehensive, "Have you been crying?"

"Yes," Lexie admitted.

"What's wrong?"

Lexie took Opal's hand and pulled her toward the sofa, "Please sit."

"What's going on, Sheriff?" Jim barked.

"I have terrible news. Jamie was found dead this afternoon."

Opal's eyes squeezed shut. Her mouth opened and closed, but no words came out.

Jim's body stiffened.

"It can't be true," Opal whimpered. "She helped weed my flower beds this morning. We're going shopping tomorrow. Jamie's buying me a new church dress—blue to match my eyes. She can't leave me. My little girl is the only one who loves me."

Disbelief erupted from Jim's mouth. "You're wrong. Jamie's strong and healthy she wouldn't drop dead."

"She was murdered."

"Murdered," Jim bellowed.

Opal's eyes widened. "No one would kill my sweet girl."

"Someone killed her, Opal, and it's my job to figure out who."

"Where is she?" Jim asked.

"At the medical examiner's office. I'll tell them to contact you as soon as her body is released for burial. Her body was found outside her car on the hill going up to Loretta's house. Did she tell you she was having lunch with Loretta today?"

Jim shook his head no.

"She told me," Opal said.

"Do you know if Jamie informed anyone else about the lunch date, or did you tell anyone?"

"I didn't tell, and I don't know whether Jamie did. However, it was late morning when Loretta phoned and asked her, so not much time to tell anyone. Jamie's not fond of her. She knew Loretta has had a tough time since her husband walked out. My good-hearted daughter went to keep her company."

"Do you know anyone who had it in for Jamie? Has she talked about threats? Anyone angry at her?"

Jim's features scrunched into hate. "You mean besides your brother?"

"Tye loved Jamie. They separated because your daughter believed your lie—which brings up another aspect of the investigation. There's a theory that Jamie died as payback for you hurting the killer's daughter. An eye for an eye scenario."

Jim's cheeks puffed. "You're blaming me for my daughter's death?"

"I don't think you killed Jamie. I think your actions provoked one of your victims or her family member to murder your child."

"If someone hated me, they'd kill me, not my innocent daughter!"

"Not necessarily. When you're dead, you're dead; you don't feel pain. When your child is dead, you feel pain and guilt for the rest of your life— a far better punishment if you think about it logically."

Opal pulled herself up using the sofa armrest. Her hands shook. "I'm going to bed. Maybe I'll wake up from this nightmare."

She stumbled forward.

"Help her Jim."

He stepped toward Opal and held her arm as they walked through a bedroom door.

He returned a minute later. He looked down into Lexie's face as he lorded over her. "I don't have any answers, but when I find out who did this, he'll die slowly."

"Not smart to tell the sheriff you're going to murder someone."

"Your word against mine, and I've got far more friends in this town than you."

Lexie pushed him back as she stood. "Are you getting any threatening calls? Has anyone confronted you about what you did to Starla?"

"You mean the entrapment?"

"I don't care what you call it. Answer my question."

"Her father left a phone message, and her boyfriend, Blake, tried to intimidate me. I cut them both down to size. No one bullies me and gets away with it—I'll break them in half."

"Which is a good reason for them to hurt your daughter instead of attacking you."

"It's possible," he admitted.

"I'm thinking it's more than possible. I'm thinking it's probable."

Jim turned his back, "I'm finished talking."

"That's fine for now. Tomorrow morning, bring me a list of girls you've molested over the last thirty or forty years. The victims or any of their family members may be your daughter's killer."

"I can't," he stammered.

"You're refusing to help solve your daughter's murder?"

"I don't remember their names."

Nausea churned Lexie's stomach. "Perhaps if you think real hard you can come up with a few names. Don't get near Gil, Dana, Starla, Gary, or Blake if you don't want locked up for harassment."

"It'd be worth jail time to smash their faces."

"Even if they're innocent? I promise I'll lock you up if you get near them."

"You missed my point Sheriff—I don't care."

"Stay clean for Opal. She'll need someone to lean on at Jamie's funeral."

Lexie didn't wait for a reply. She left without condolence. She heard a pained yelp as she crossed the front porch. Apparently, the news had finally registered in Jim's heart.

Much work is left, but my day is far too long already. I'll pick up Sky and hope that we'll sleep tonight.

CHAPTER TWENTY-NINE

The Jeep lunged forward when Tye stomped the brakes in front of his mom's house. He'd get the boys and leave fast.

Lexie texted that she'd told Mom about the death so he didn't have to deal with her reaction. Lexie also told her to let Tye tell his sons. He'd do that in the quiet of their home. He'd wait until tomorrow so they'd have a good sleep tonight.

Gabriel ran toward him as he entered the living room. "What happened to Mommy? Grandma said she was killed. Who hurt her, Daddy?"

Tye scooped the boy into a hug. "We're going home, son. We'll talk about your mommy later."

Over Gabriel's shoulder, Tye's eyes shot daggers at his mother.

"Someone had to tell them," Margo defended.

His words fired back, "That was my job."

"Well, I saved you the trouble."

Seth hung back in the corner, silent.

Tye's mind flashed back to when Seth's biological mother died. The boy said only a few isolated words for weeks. Now—again—he'd lost a mother.

Tye beckoned, "Come here, Seth."

The boy remained statue still. Tye moved toward him and wrapped his stiff body in his arms. "We have each other, and we'll get through this together."

Gabriel sniffled, "What if you die, Daddy?"

"I won't die until I'm a grouchy old man."

"Where will we go when you die? Grandma doesn't like us."

"You'll live with Aunt Lexie if anything happens to me."

Gabriel squinted, "What if she doesn't want us?"

"I asked her long ago. She said it was a stupid question since she loved you both with all her heart."

Margo piped in, "That'd be tough since she's single and has her hands full with Sky."

Tye turned his angry face, "Shut up, just shut up."

Margo's hand pressed her chest, "Well, I never."

"Yep you never thought about how your words make it harder for my sons."

"I speak the truth. Even if it hurts."

"Get your backpacks guys, let's go home."

In the Jeep, Gabriel asked, "Does Adam know?"

"Your Aunt Lexie phoned him. He'll come home from college soon."

"I have homework," Gabriel remembered.

"Tomorrow we'll stay home and plan your mom's funeral. Seth, what are those flowers that your mom likes?"

"Daisies—she likes daisies—I mean liked."

"That's what we'll get for her."

"She could wear her blue church dress," Gabriel suggested. "Her shoes hurt her feet."

Seth's bottom lip quivered, "Dead people don't need shoes."

Tye agreed, "We'll put house slippers on with her blue dress. No one will see her feet."

Gabrielle giggled, "Good idea, Daddy."

Seth stared out the window.

I'll contact the psychologist who worked with him after his biological mom died.

The darkness hid the tears welling in Tye's eyes. Deep inside his sorrow grew—he feared it would consume his entire being if he didn't find a way to control it.

CHAPTER THIRTY

Lexie awoke with a sinking feeling. It took a few seconds to realize why. Jamie was gone forever—dead. She heard footsteps running down the hall before she saw Sky's face peek around the doorway.

"I want pancakes, Mommy."

"I'll have to cook the toaster kind, honey. No time to mix them from scratch this morning. How about cereal today, and we'll make pancakes on Saturday?"

"Okay."

"Sit on my bed and look at your book while I take a shower."

Lexie splashed warm water on her face. She hoped the water would activate her body left numb from two or three hours of sleep. Soon she'd tell Sky that Aunt Jamie was dead, but she couldn't do it now. There was no time to fall apart before work. A note handed to the day care worker would convey that she'd tell Sky after work. Tonight, she'd find a way to tell her little daughter.

———— • ————

The childcare worker read the note then hugged Lexie. She gave Sky a quick kiss and rushed out the door before the emotions building in her chest erupted.

The cell phone played its tune as she turned the key in the ignition.

"What's happening, Lexie?"

"Stan?"

"Yep, it's me. The man you rejected then negotiated for friendship instead of hot sex."

"Glad you remember our relationship status."

The low masculine voice taunted. "Your loss, girlfriend."

"Do you have a purpose for this call other than harassment?"

"I heard about your brother's wife."

"In Washington, D.C.?"

"News travels fast when someone in law enforcement has a murdered spouse. How's the case moving?"

"Highway patrol handled the site investigation. I'll get a report on their findings this morning. They put me on the sideline since my relative was murdered. Of course, they always look at the husband first when a wife dies."

Stan mumbled, "I don't want to offend you…"

"That's a first," she teased.

"Very funny. Any chance your brother was involved? Like I said, no offense."

"He worked a car accident an hour or so before lunch which is when the murder occurred. Jamie had a noon lunch date with a friend. She was shot beside the road."

"Sounds legit. Ruling your brother out is a necessity."

"I know."

"Is he working?" Stan inquired.

"Called in today. He's spending the day with his boys. I don't expect him back until after the funeral. He's devastated."

"You're short-handed?"

"Always, but now this emotional upheaval took Tye away from work. It'll be a trick to get everything done."

Stan's next words were matter-of-fact. "I'll fly out and help you investigate."

"I can't ask you to use your vacation days."

"You didn't ask—I told you. I'll assist my girl pal."

A thought clicked in Lexie's head. "You realize there are no fringe benefits?"

"I'm being accused of an ulterior motive?" He sounded offended.

"Based on our history, don't sound so surprised. Anyway, this is really too generous."

"Too late, girlfriend, I already bought my plane ticket. I'll rent a car and arrive this afternoon. Assuming you won't share your bed, will you find me a place to stay for three or four nights?"

"I'll do it—thanks so much."

Lexie said good-bye as relief replaced work anguish in her brain. Now J.J. can stay on night shift. Sloan can continue to monitor phone calls at night. Stan can sub for Tye. Stan's a blessing unless he forgets we're just friends and resumes his past sexual pursuit.

———— ♦ ————

Dana ran down her front steps as Lexie opened the gate.

"I'm late to work, Sheriff."

"I'll catch you later. I'm looking for your ex-husband. Where is he?"

She talked as she sped toward her car. "He's staying with his brother—another low life. They're on Elm—the shack beside the filling station—he owns both. Got to go."

Dana didn't ask what was going on, but she didn't seem nervous just in a hurry.

Stops at the filling station and the shack resulted in no response and locked doors.

Lexie thought about dropping by Diffee High, but she'd have to inform Blake's parents before interviewing him.

A text from Delia revealed her next business. Houser ordered Lexie to his office ASAP.

CHAPTER THIRTY-ONE

Perhaps Houser's site investigation pointed to Jamie's killer.

Lexie felt sorrow ebbing through her "stay tough" resolve as she drove toward the Highway Patrol office. No, she told herself. I can't get emotional. I've got to solve this case for Tye.

---◆---

Houser rose when Lexie entered the room. His usual gruff facial expression was softened by the concern in his eyes. "I'm sorry tragedy struck your family. How's Tye holding up?"

"You know Tye—he doesn't let that tough-guy exterior crack."

He motioned toward a chair. "I've seen even the hardest men crack when they lose a wife or child."

Lexie sat at the cushion's edge. "I have no doubt it's taking all the strength he has to hold himself together."

"Give me a report of your findings."

She pulled notes from her case. "I'll give you a rundown, although I'm not far along. I informed Jim and Opal Evans of Jamie's death. They didn't have any insights as to anyone who might want Jamie dead. Jim pointed a finger at Tye since he and Jamie recently separated. I told him I suspected the killer was a family member of one of the young women he molested."

"How did he respond to that accusation?"

"He acknowledged that it was a possibility. I asked for a list of the girls he'd molested. He claimed that he didn't remember their names."

Houser's face clouded, "What a piece of shit."

"He's supposed to drop off a list of those he remembers."

"You know, Sheriff, that'll never happen. He won't admit anything."

"You'd think a dead daughter might motivate him to become a better man."

"Nothing makes those perverts better," Houser scoffed.

"Principal Bradford said Jamie received negative feedback as a result of the accusations against her father. It's easier to bully Jamie for her father's sins than confront him directly. What have you learned?"

"The site investigation ruled out suicide, which was a no-brainer, but necessary. The star-shaped pattern on the entry wound indicated that she was shot at close range."

Lexie leaned forward, "Any defensive wounds?"

"None, which means she knew her killer."

"Robbery?"

"Your sister-in-law's purse was on the front seat. Wallet was intact with $150 cash. Wedding ring was still on her finger. Robbery obviously wasn't the motive."

"Car tracks or broken foliage?" Lexie questioned.

Houser pulled at his chin. "Ground is rock and dirt—no indication that a car parked on the road. My guys examined a 200-yard parameter. They didn't find any evidence. I always hope the killer will drop a personal item or leave a shell casing behind, but we didn't get lucky. The medical examiner did find a hair on Jamie's body before he bagged and tagged her body."

"Is the hair at the lab?"

"Yes. The examiner will also check for touch DNA in case the killer had the desire to get close for a final good-bye."

"Sounds sick and creepy."

"Blood splatter indicated a thirty-five to forty-five degree angle, which means Jamie didn't die immediately. There was also blood splatter in the driver's door well. Apparently, Jamie got out and stood with the door open."

Lexie thought aloud, "So the killer flagged her down, and she opened the door to talk?"

"Likely he pretended some kind of distress to coax her into his web."

Lexie rubbed her hands together. "What I'm trying to figure out is how the killer knew about Jamie's luncheon date."

"That's certainly a valid question. The answer may break open the case."

"The killer was lying in wait. He knew where she was going. Jamie's mom said Loretta didn't invite Jamie until 10 o'clock yesterday morning. Opal didn't tell anyone."

Houser continued the line of thought. "But someone told the killer and that's who we need to identify."

"I'll interview Loretta again. She freaked yesterday."

"Sounds like a good place to begin," Houser acknowledged.

"The father of the most recent girl Jim molested is a person of interest. I'll pursue that lead today. Thanks for your information, Houser."

"You know where to find me."

"I do."

---·---

Lexie's heart raced as she passed Jamie's murder site on the way to Loretta's house. The familiar car parked out front sent ripples of irritation through her body.

The front door swung open and she came eye to eye with Margo. "What are you doing here, Mom?"

"I'm visiting my friend," she snapped. "This Jamie thing is hard on Loretta."

Lexie shrugged, "Where is she?"

"In the master bedroom. I'm styling her hair. She's let herself go since that no-good husband left her." Margo whispered in Lexie's ear, "She's gotten very attached to the bottle—if you know what I mean."

Loretta sat on the corner of an unmade bed. Half her hair was hot curled. The other half lay in wait for Margo.

Loretta stared at her hands. "Have you found Jamie's killer?"

"Not yet—I have more questions. Did you finish a list of everyone you told about the luncheon date with Jamie?"

"It's too much work."

"It's TOO MUCH work to find your friend's killer?" Lexie yelled.

Margo reprimanded, "Don't sound so abrasive."

Lexie pulled out a notepad. "Tell me the names and I'll write them down."

Loretta manipulated her i-Pad. "Here's my home page and a list of my Facebook friends—all 253 of them."

A sinking feeling invaded Lexie's hope. "You put on Facebook that Jamie was having lunch with you and the time?"

"I always tell Facebook friends my plans."

"One of your friends probably used your post to schedule Jamie's death."

"You're blaming me?" Loretta scolded.

Margo gave Lexie a steely look and patted Loretta's back. "Of course, it's not your fault. You had no way of knowing. Get out, Lexie. You've upset her."

"You can't dismiss a sheriff, Mother, even though I'm your daughter."

"Tell Tye to interview her. They've been friends for years."

"What are you up to?"

Margo rolled a hair section in the curling iron. "I'm trying to restore her, and you're tearing her down."

"I'm attempting to solve a murder case."

Margo waved her off, "Tell your brother to interview Loretta—you're his boss."

"My brother is in mourning—a widower."

"Well, he doesn't need to mope around very long."

Lexie turned away to gain composure, "Why is that?"

Margo's red lips stretched into a smile. "Because he's single and Loretta's single and they'll make the perfect couple."

"You really don't know your son."

"I will never understand how a daughter of mine turned out so spiteful."

Lexie changed the subject to control her desire to slap her mother. "Loretta, I heard the room off your back porch is for rent. I'd like to reserve it for a colleague who'll assist with the investigation."

"It's $100 a night."

"How about $60 since he's helping with Jamie's case."

"Anything for Jamie."

"I'll bring Stan over later today. If you think of additional case information call me."

Loretta didn't respond. Margo continued styling her hair without a glance in Lexie's direction.

Lexie purposely slammed the front door as she exited—a loud noise conveying disgust. She knew the sound and feeling were lost on the two women upstairs.

CHAPTER THIRTY-TWO

Diffee High was Lexie's next stop. She'd scheduled a meeting with Blake, Starla's boyfriend, and his mother. She found the pair waiting in Bradford's office with Cecil Lansbury.

"They don't require an attorney, Cecil. Unless of course they know something I don't."

"We have rights," the teen's mom announced.

"Yes," Cecil agreed, "I'll monitor your conversation."

"Where were you yesterday, Blake, between 10 o'clock and noon?"

The boy clinched the chair arms, "At school."

"Who were you with over the lunch hour?"

"Jake, Damien, and I ate at the burger joint across the street."

Lexie pointed at his face. "I heard you had words with Coach Evans."

"He was messing with my girl." Blake's fist pressed against his cheek, "I told the pervert to bug off."

"What was his response?"

"Speaking of bugs, he'd crush me like a roach under his boot if I didn't back off."

Lexie continued, "What happened next?"

"The owner of the hardware store told me to get out. He'd have no young punk picking a fight in his place."

"What did Starla say about your confrontation with Coach?"

"She said her daddy would handle Evans."

"How was her daddy going to do that?"

"She didn't tell me. She did say it was time Gil acted like a father."

"Are you charging this boy?" Cecil inquired.

"There's no reason at this point in time." Lexie focused on the mother. "Keep your son under your thumb until I catch this killer."

"Why?" she asked.

"If Coach Evans thinks your son had any part in Jamie's death he'll become a target. You can leave now."

On the way out the door, the mother grounded her son for two weeks.

"Mr. Bradford, will you bring those two boys that Blake mentioned in individually? See if they'll confirm his story. Also, check with his teachers to make sure he attended classes before lunch."

"I'll get on it as soon as you leave," Bradford assured.

"I appreciate your help."

———— • ————

Lexie glanced at her watch as she walked down the high school steps. The hardware store owner's questioning can wait until tomorrow. Stan was due in her office in a few minutes, and she'd forgotten to tell Delia. She met Stan years ago and immediately despised him.

When she reached the office, she found the pair sitting in strained silence.

"Sorry I didn't inform you that Stan's subbing for Tye until after the funeral."

Delia words squeezed out, "Wish I was warned. The paperwork isn't ready. It's about quitting time. Sloan and I have church tonight."

Lexie didn't miss the huffiness. "Go home, tomorrow morning is soon enough."

Delia disappeared out the door as if a fire was lit under her ass.

Stan wrapped his arms around Lexie and planted a kiss on her lips as Red walked in the door.

"Sorry," Red blurted. "I have bad timing. Dropped by to find out what I can do for Tye. He's not answering his phone."

Heat invaded Lexie's body and sweat erupted on her forehead. "Red, this is Detective Stan Johnson. He volunteered to serve as a deputy while Tye is off."

Contempt hardened Red's tone. "I remember how he put our friend in jail for a murder he didn't commit."

Stan's eyes shot daggers. Red didn't break the stare.

Lexie's words stumbled out, "Best if you drop by Tye's house and ask him directly."

"I'll do that."

Red left and Lexie lit into Stan. "What was that kiss about? Did you forget that we're friends not lovers?"

"At any moment you may change your mind. I'm always up for a relationship upgrade."

"Am I the only woman who ever refused to sleep with you? I'm part of your game hunt—can't admit failure? I'm not a person—I'm a sexual target?"

"Cut the drama. You're bent out of shape because your old lover showed up at the wrong time. I'm hung up on pursuing you, and you're obsessed with a married man."

She didn't share that Red filed for divorce.

Stan was abrupt, "Give me a summary of your case and what we need to do."

Lexie motioned toward the conference table. She reviewed Houser's findings and the interviews she'd conducted. "I think it's a dead end, but I'll talk to Rick, the hardware store owner, to be sure his report coincides with Blake's. I'll phone Principal Bradford in the morning to find out if Blake's alibi held."

"Sounds like you're convinced this case is tied in with Jim's deviant behavior?"

"That's where I'm leaning, but I hope it's not blinding me to a different motive."

"Who are we questioning tomorrow?"

"Our main suspect is Gil Jenkins—Starla's father. She's the most recent girl Jim molested. I received a report that he threatened Jim. Gil has a criminal history and guilt."

"Guilt?"

"He deserted Starla's mom and played no role in their child's upbringing. Now he has returned and is playing protective daddy."

"How is Starla's mom reacting to him hanging around?"

"I think he wants Dana back, but she's not falling into his arms."

Stan paced, "So she isn't likely to protect him?"

"I don't think so. I'd like you to handle Gary King's interview. He's Abbey's husband, the woman who died on my watch. We had another altercation when his son died as a result of Shaken Baby Syndrome. As soon as he sees my face, he becomes hostile—with good reason."

Stan leaned against the file cabinet. "He's a suspect because he hates you?"

"I hadn't thought of that perspective. But no—he's a person of interest because he confronted Jim. Gary feared his daughter, Megan, was abused by the coach."

"Anyone else on our agenda?"

"A conversation with Dana might be of interest."

"Sounds like we have a plan."

"I rented Loretta's servant quarters for you. It's a nice bedroom with an attached bath. It's close to the murder site. Loretta is the one who found Jamie; perhaps you can get her talking. She may have information that she hasn't shared with me."

"Sounds like a good idea. I'll walk the crime scene before dark. Sometimes a new pair of eyes sees things that others miss."

"Let's head that way. Follow me in your rental car. I'll honk as we pass the murder site. First, I'll phone in a supper order for you from Dixie's."

"You're not going to eat dinner with me?"

"I'm sorry—no time—Sky's day care closes at 5:30."

"That's a plan," Stan said, "but not the one I hoped for."

CHAPTER THIRTY-THREE

"Where's Delia?" Stan asked when he entered Lexie's office at 8 o'clock the next morning.

"She'll arrive in a few minutes. She had a flat tire."

"I don't miss her evil eye," he admitted.

"She hasn't gotten over you jailing her hometown boy."

"Seems like she could try that Christian thing—forgive and forget."

"Learn anything from Loretta?"

Stan smiled from ear to ear.

Lexie's hand pressed her forehead. "Please don't tell me you had sex with someone involved in our case."

"There's one thing more important than sex—that's getting the bad guys. I don't have personal involvements with anyone in active cases. I'm insulted that you would assume I would."

"That's good news, but why do you have that cat-ate-the-canary look on your face?"

"I did a good deed last night. Loretta's ex-husband showed up at her door with his, very pregnant, snooty girlfriend. He'd left clothes behind when he fled. Loretta started whimpering as soon as she saw them through the front window. I told her to brush her hair and get her act together while I let them in. No wailing or blaming allowed and to act like she didn't give a damn."

"Did she follow directions?"

"Yes, she did. Boy was the guy surprised when I answered the door." Stan fidgeted with his cell phone.

"Don't leave me in suspense, tell me what happened," Lexie urged.

"'Who are you?' I asked. He said Sam Wells, Loretta's ex-husband, and then he asked who I was. I identified myself as his replacement. Told him I'd check to see if Loretta wanted him in her house."

Lexie's eyes bugged, "I bet that set him off."

"Sam snarled, 'I paid for this house.' I thanked him for his contribution to our happiness. His pregnant companion giggled. 'Honey,' I called, 'some guy is here to pick-up his junk.' Loretta then walked down the steps with every hair in place and a gown cut to her navel. The guy's face paled. Her hand squeezed my upper arm as she spoke. 'Your clothes are in the front closet, Sam. Get them and get out. We're busy.'"

Lexie patted his back. "You're a nice guy after all."

"After he left, she kissed my cheek. She said it was the best she'd felt since he walked out."

"Nothing better than parading a hunk in front of your cheating ex-husband."

"So you think I'm a hunk?"

"As far as I'm concerned, your obnoxious comments pretty much cancel out your good looks."

"Damn, I rescue your friend and you still treat me like crap."

"Loretta's not really my friend, but I appreciate you giving her some power. Did you get any new case insights?"

"We walked the site before dark. She didn't say anything you hadn't already told me. She broke down and ran in her bedroom as soon as we got back up the hill."

She handed him a sheet of paper. "Here are the directions to Gary's farm."

"Do you really think he's a suspect?"

"I doubt it, but he's experienced much family loss over the last few years. There's a chance he'd play an eye for an eye if he thought someone hurt Megan."

"Where are you headed?"

"I'll question Rick Barney, the hardware store owner. Then I'll check with Principal Bradford regarding Blake's alibi. Return here when you're finished with Gary. We'll find Gil together."

"That works for me, boss."

Lexie followed Stan out the door. She walked three blocks on Main Street to the hardware store. The green grass and flowers made her realize the beauty of spring had arrived, even though her family was shadowed in darkness.

Barney's Hardware Haven housed bolts, fixtures, and more for forty years. In spite of the store's lack of organization, Barney was able to put his hands on anything a person requested within three minutes. A bell announced Lexie's entrance into his gadget world.

Barney's calloused hands disappeared into his overall pockets. "What are you looking for today, Sheriff?"

"Information."

"That's not profitable."

"Sorry about that. I'll buy a new weedwhacker as soon as the weeds start taking over my fence."

Barney walked toward a display, "I have a good selection."

"I received a report that you heard Jim Evans and Blake argue."

"That's true."

"Run through their conversation so I can verify the information I received."

"Coach Jim bought filters for his air conditioner. Just happened that kid was in the back aisle looking for bolts for his dad. The kid got in Coach's face and told him to leave Starla alone or he'd be sorry."

"What did Coach say?"

"Told him to back off then go to hell. Claimed Starla was a lying whore and the boy should stay clear of her."

"Did Coach threaten Blake?"

"He defended himself."

"Coach didn't say he'd crush the teen under his shoe like a roach?"

Barney's gaze wandered, "Coach responded to what the kid said to him—it wasn't a threat."

"That's a matter of opinion."

"Boy had no respect for his elder. He was put in his place."

"That's all my questions for now. Have a good day."

"Come buy your weedwhacker soon."

Lexie didn't respond. At the moment, conducting business with someone who defended Jim wasn't appealing.

She pushed Bradford's number into her phone as she walked.

"What did the boys tell you, Mr. Bradford?"

"They named their lunch partners. Blake was on both lists. His teachers confirmed he was in English at 10 o'clock and Geometry at 11 o'clock."

"Looks like his alibi is tight."

"He's a good kid. I didn't think for a minute he'd get involved in a murder."

"I had to check it out due to the report that Blake threatened Jim because he hurt Starla."

Bradford nodded, "I know you're doing your job."

"Thanks for the help."

"You're welcome."

The smell of coffee greeted Lexie when she entered her office.

"Sloan fix your flat?"

"Tire was too far gone. He bought me a new one. Sorry I'm late."

"No big deal. Stan will return soon. He's questioning Gary King."

Delia made a sour face. "That Stan guy gives me the creeps."

"You do the same to him. He said that you gave him the evil eye."

Delia pulled at her ear lobe. "He deserved the evil eye."

"Stan also hoped you'd follow the Christian practice of forgiveness." Lexie knew her bluntness stung, but Delia had no business making any of the Sheriff's associates uncomfortable.

"I never considered forgiveness for that cocky dude. You like him?"

"It doesn't matter what either of us think of him. He came here because we're short-handed. We should appreciate his contributions."

"I promise I'll do better."

"I'd appreciate it."

Twenty minutes later, Delia sang out a strained, "Good morning" when Stan entered the room.

"Good day to you, Delia."

"Let's talk in my office," Lexie directed.

Stan settled in a chair. "Why did Delia speak to me?"

"Because her boss suggested that she act civil to someone who's helping us solve a murder."

"Ah, you're my heroine—defending my honor."

"Something like that. The high school boys confirmed Blake's alibi. He's off my suspect list. Is Gary still on that list?"

"He was at work all that day, and, yes, I confirmed with his supervisor. He did say you use him as a perpetual person of interest."

"Did he admit to confronting Jim?"

"He believed Jim when he said Starla was a little tart who made up the story. Megan denied that Evans was inappropriate with her. Megan confirmed to her father, with me present, that Starla has a bad reputation."

Lexie pulled at her braid. "Not possible everyone on our list is innocent. Let's figure out if Gil Jenkins is the guilty one."

CHAPTER THIRTY-FOUR

Starla opened the door at Lexie's request.

"Where's your mom?"

"At work."

"Why aren't you at school?"

Starla rolled her eyes. "Did you forget I'm the whore who seduced beloved Coach Evans?"

"I'm surprised," Lexie responded. "You don't seem like the type who'd let other people rule your life."

"I'm tough, not stupid."

Gil sat in a corner recliner taking in the conversation. "Why are you hounding my daughter? She's the victim in all your mess."

"We're not here for Starla. We're here to question you."

Gil pointed toward Stan, "Who's that?"

"Detective Stan Johnson. I'm assisting the sheriff since her brother is in mourning. I'm sure you know someone murdered his wife."

A twisted smile parted Gil's lips. "I'm aware Evans lost his only child to violence. It's perfect retribution for a man who rapes teenagers."

"I heard you threatened Jim."

"That's true, but Evans is the one I planned to hurt, not his daughter."

"I can think of nothing that hurts Jim more than the pain of losing Jamie."

Gil snorted, "That means someone was successful. I'd like to pat that guy's back."

Lexie leaned her face into his, "Are you the successful one? Did you fulfill your promise to Starla? Did you make her abuser pay?"

Gil sat silently. His eyes studied the ceiling.

Stan kicked his shoe, "Does your silence mean you killed Jamie?"

"Back off, Johnson. I didn't answer because I have nothing to confess."

Lexie's stare pierced into his eyes. "You're not denying you killed Jamie Wolfe?"

"Maybe I did. Maybe I didn't. Regardless, he deserved punishment for hurting my little girl. Now Starla's dropped out of school—he screwed up her life."

"After eighteen years, you've become a good daddy?" Stan remarked.

"Better late than never, and never is coming fast."

"What does that mean, Gil?"

"I have stage four prostate cancer. I came back to tell Starla that I'm sorry I've been a no-account father."

Stan's facial muscles tightened. "Logic tells me that you showed your sudden love and support by killing the daughter of the man who hurt yours."

Gil snapped his fingers. "Something a good dad would do; don't you agree?"

Lexie unbuckled the handcuffs from her belt. "Sounds like a confession."

Starla's stance widened, her hands on her waist. "Dad didn't confess to anything. Don't put words in his mouth."

"Good dads don't murder innocent people."

"Maybe they would, Sheriff, if they loved their daughters enough."

Stan confronted, "He's trying to earn your love by playing protector—something he's never been in your life."

"You don't know my father."

Lexie interjected, "I know he spent most of your childhood in prison. He fooled around with another woman when your mother was pregnant with you. That's your daddy—a criminal—an adulterer—a deadbeat father."

"None of that matters now," Starla defended.

"Gil, where were you Thursday morning?"

"I have trouble remembering when I do what. These cancer meds impact my memory."

Lexie rattled the handcuffs. "Again, did you murder Jamie Evans Wolfe?"

"I'm not confessing, Sheriff, find your own evidence. I'm not sending myself back to prison to die."

Stan fisted the front of Gil's shirt and pulled him to standing. "I don't like games, and I guarantee you're not winning this one."

"Let's go Stan," Lexie ordered.

"Yeah, Stan," Gil teased, "follow your boss girl."

The cruiser sped toward her office. Lexie had no idea why she was in a hurry. Perhaps she was escaping from the frustration with Gil as soon as possible.

"Lexie, what do you make of that nut?"

"I've never come into contact with a suspect like him. He was on the verge of confessing then backed down—he enjoyed playing us."

"Any evidence he committed the murder?"

"Nothing yet. If the hair on Jamie's body doesn't come back with his DNA, he'll die a free man."

Scowl lines formed in Stan's forehead. "Why would he lead us to suspect him? Most criminals lie, beg, and cry to convince us they're innocent. Gil did the opposite. He wants us to think he did it, but why?"

She spent a few moments in thought. "Perhaps because he's trying to protect the person who actually committed the crime—Starla or Dana. If we arrest one of the two, I bet he'll confess."

"Would Jamie have stopped on the road for Starla?"

"She was in Jamie's class so they knew each other. She would've stopped for any girl waving for help. That's who she is—was."

"You think Starla is the killer," Stan concluded.

"That's where I'm leaning. I don't see Dana as emotionally warped enough to murder an innocent woman. If my Starla theory is correct Gil isn't the killer. He's setting up a way to take her place if she's charged. Then there's the theory that his interactions with us was a performance to lead Starla to believe that he'd risk his freedom to protect her—kill for her. He may not have murdered Jamie, but he wants Starla to think he did."

"You think he's playing hero daddy?"

"A real possibility," Lexie acknowledged.

"What's our next move, Sheriff?"

"I'll phone Dana at work and tell her to bring Starla and meet us at the office around 4 o'clock."

"We need to know if Starla has an alibi."

"Exactly. By the way, Dana is gorgeous so try to keep your focus on the case and not her private parts."

"I resent that snide comment. As I've already told you sex is always second to solving cases."

"That's the only good news I've heard today."

"Sheriff comedian—unfortunately you're not funny."

CHAPTER THIRTY-FIVE

Tye glanced out the kitchen window. Seth and Gabriel played catch in the back yard. *Maybe I should've taken them to school today, but I'll wait until after the funeral. The kids might ask them too many questions.*

Seth was quiet much of the time, and Gabriel wasn't his usual inquisitive self. Tye felt enveloped in a cloud of darkness. Sometimes he forgot Jamie was gone. This morning he'd called out her name when he thought she was in the bathroom. Soon he realized he left the light on overnight. He grabbed a book, a mug, pillows, and the alarm clock and took aim at the empty room.

Seth's yell stopped his bombardment. The red-eyed boy stood in the doorway. "Are you hurt, Daddy?"

"No, son, I'm angry because your mama died. I'm mad because there are terrible people in the world who take lives and destroy happiness. I'm sorry I frightened you."

"I'm angry, Daddy. May I throw something?"

Tye pulled two books from the nightstand and handed them to his son. "Go for it!"

Seth heaved with all his might. The first book crashed into the front of the dresser. The second book hit the mirror, sending a kaleidoscope of cracks across its surface. He cried out, "I'm sorry, Daddy."

The pair stood in front of the broken glass, their reflections cracked. "Look at us all cracked and broken. It'll take time to get better, but, like the dresser, we'll be whole again. You set the table for breakfast and pour the cereal while I take a shower."

Tye thought Seth was more animated after the mirror incident. He was the one who took Gabriel out to play. Perhaps it's good to see the cracks when your heart is broken.

A voice called from the living room. "Where are you, Tye?"

He looked longingly at the broom closet—a place to hide. "I'm in the kitchen, Mom."

"You look terrible. Are you sleeping at all?"

"I'm having a bad week," sarcasm dripped from his words.

"This, too, shall pass," Margo quipped.

Anger boiled in Tye's brain. "Jamie's life will never pass from my memory. What are you doing here?"

Seth and Gabriel stormed in the back door.

"Slow down," Margo warned, "you two are like wild animals."

Gabriel ignored his grandmother. "May we have popsicles?"

"Eat them at the kitchen table," Tye directed.

Margo set a bag on the table. "Look what I bought for your mom to wear in her casket." She pulled out a lacey, pale pink dress.

Gabriel's voice peaked, "Mama hates pink."

"It's beautiful, and she's dead. She'll not care about the color."

Tye wondered how his mother knew Jamie for years and didn't know that she had no use for pink frills. "Thanks for the thought, but we already picked Jamie's dress."

Seth responded enthusiastically, "It's blue—Mama's favorite color,"

"Where did you buy it?"

"It was her favorite church dress," Tye answered.

"Don't bury her in an old dress. What a travesty. The neighbors will gossip."

Gabriel giggled, "We're going to put house shoes on her feet."

Margo vehemently shook her head. "Oh, Tye—please don't—how embarrassing."

Tye's tone left no room for argument. "We're sending her off with what she liked on earth. That's more than respect—it's love."

Margo's breath sucked in. "Has your sister found the killer?"

"No, but she will."

"A newspaper article said the evidence isn't pointing to a specific person. The reporter claimed the case might never get solved."

"Let's not talk about the case. This conversation is too painful for your grandsons."

Margo reprimanded, "You must stop sulking and move on."

"There's no place I want to go without Jamie."

Margo's chin rose, "I'll take this beautiful dress back. I wanted everyone to see how much Jamie meant to us."

"The best help you can give, Mom, is to act as hostess when people show up here after the funeral."

Her eyes surveyed the kitchen, "This place is a mess."

"The boys and I will clean this afternoon. Will you buy paper products and snacks?" Tye reached for his wallet.

"Heavens, I don't want your money. Church people bring plenty of food, and I'll get the paper products."

"Thanks."

"You're welcome." She kissed his cheek then hurried out the door toward her hostess mission.

"Boys, your grandma was right about one thing: Our house is dirty. First, get all the toys in your room. Second, Seth vacuums while Gabriel dusts. I'll scrub the bathrooms while you two finish your chores. You have marching orders so go to it!"

Gabriel brought up his knees alternately as he moved toward the toys.

"That's what I'm talking about," Tye almost smiled.

CHAPTER THIRTY-SIX

Stan stood in the office doorway awaiting the arrival of Dana and Starla.

He called over his shoulder, "You're right, Dana is hot."

"So they have arrived?"

"Almost."

Stan held the door open as the mother and daughter entered.

Lexie noted that Dana always looked unkempt and depressed when she saw her at home. She'd been at work, which resulted in a transformation to a gorgeous career woman.

Lexie didn't miss the pause then smile on Dana's lips as she responded to Stan's "hello."

"Ladies, this is Detective Stan Johnson, who is serving as a short-term deputy during the investigation of Jamie Wolfe's death."

Dana's friendliness disappeared, "That death has nothing to do with Starla or myself. Why did you order us here?"

"It's important that you understand that if either of you are withholding evidence in Jamie's case, you'll face prosecution. Starla's punishment would be the same as any other adult."

"Mrs. Wolfe was Starla's favorite teacher. We have no reason to kill her or know who did."

"My theory is that someone murdered Jamie because of her father's perverted behavior. You both have reason to hate Coach Evans."

Dana shrugged, "I can't deny that I hate the man, but I don't murder people."

Lexie eyed Starla, "Gil almost confessed to the murder. I'm concerned that your daughter knows he committed the crime and is now an accessory."

Dana turned to her daughter, "Did Gil tell you he killed Mrs. Wolfe?"

"No!" Starla snapped. "Sheriff heard the same thing I heard. He never said he killed anyone."

"But he implied he did," Stan added.

Lexie stepped into Starla's personal space. "Maybe he thinks you killed Jamie. He's made himself look like a suspect in case he needs to save you later."

Dana's words blurted out, "You're accusing my daughter of murder?"

"I'm trying to figure out why Gil aimed the suspicion at himself if he didn't commit the crime."

"Trust me," Dana said, "I have no insight as to what the jerk does or why."

"Where were you Thursday morning between 10 o'clock and noon?"

"I was at work."

"Where were you, Starla?"

"At home—alone—watching television. I bet you're happy that I don't have an alibi."

Lexie picked up a kit from her desk. "I'd like DNA samples, so I can rule both of you out as suspects. Will you voluntarily give the samples?"

Dana clutched her purse. "I'll consult with an attorney before I give you anything."

The pair gone, Stan paced. "I think Dana is afraid her daughter committed the murder."

Lexie stuck the kits back in the cabinet. "The fact she wouldn't agree to DNA testing implies that you're correct."

"There's the chance the mom and dad are both trying to protect Starla. That further substantiates her guilt."

Delia interrupted, "One of Houser's men delivered the box on your desk."

"Did he say what's in it?"

"It's the contents of Jamie's car."

"Okay, I'll take care of it. Delia, don't come in before Jamie's funeral in the morning. J.J. will relieve me at midnight. Stan will cover the morning shift."

Delia pulled her purse from a drawer. "Sky may spend the night with me if you want."

"Red volunteered to keep her tonight. He'll drop her off at day care before coming to the funeral."

"What about his baby?"

"She's still in the hospital. He said Sky lifted his spirits."

"I'll see you at the church."

"Bye," Lexie said.

"Take a dinner break, Stan, while I check the box contents. When you return please man the office phone while I visit Tye."

"That works for me. I'll hurry back."

Lexie sat at her desk and stripped away the tape that locked the box. She pulled out one item at a time: a phone, Gabriel's sock, a yo-yo, an iPad, lip-gloss, brush, a pen, wallet, and miscellaneous receipts.

Slamming desk drawers didn't eliminate her sadness or frustration. She'd lost the only sister she'd ever had. The killer would remain free for the rest of his evil life if she didn't solve the case.

Lexie plugged in Jamie's phone and iPad. She hoped the killer left a threat or a clue on a device. Maybe Jamie inadvertently phoned the killer and told him when she'd travel a deserted road.

When Stan returned, Lexie grabbed her keys and headed to Tye's house for a short visit.

CHAPTER THIRTY-SEVEN

Lexie bought pizza on her way to Tye's house. Busy with the case the last three days, she'd had only one brief conversation with her brother. His voice sounded strained as if it took more energy than he possessed to carry on a conversation.

The boys took ownership of the pizza box when she entered the house.

"We'll get the table ready," Gabriel assured her.

Dark circles and bags highlighted her brother's eyes. She wrapped a hug around him.

"Any suspects, Sis?"

"We're working the case. We ruled out most people of interest. There are a couple of suspicious characters."

"Tell me who," he prompted.

"It's too soon for that."

"You afraid I'll force a confession with hands around his neck or a knife to his heart?"

"That crossed my mind. The main problem with two suspects—you may attack the wrong one. I'm sure you don't want an innocent person harmed."

"Maybe I wouldn't care if I got the guilty one too."

"Come and eat," Seth called.

A wave of nausea disturbed her stomach as she became aware of the strangeness of Jamie's kitchen without her present. She noted that her brother wasn't eating. His sons ate slowly.

"Nephews, are you on the cleaning crew? Place looks shiny."

"Daddy said Mama always wanted the house spic and span for company so we'd better make her proud," Seth informed.

"I have no doubt she'd be very proud, and I am, too."

"Grandma was mad because Mommy is wearing her house shoes at the funeral."

Lexie finished chewing as she looked at Gabriel. "I don't understand."

"Mommy liked soft shoes, so we decided she should wear her house slippers. Grandma was pissed."

Lexie grinned, "That's what I'd want to wear."

"There's a little sunlight left, guys. We'll visit while you play outside for a few minutes. After you come back in, we'll clean your bedroom."

The boys ran out the back door.

Lexie shut the door behind them, "How are they doing?"

"A little better than I expected. Seth is talking some, and Gabriel is quieter but still inquisitive. There was one incident."

"What happened?"

"Gabriel fell when the guys played outside earlier today. He ran in with a bloody knee. He cried out, 'Mommy, Mommy.' He looked at my face and broke into sobs. All three of us cried while I cleaned the cut."

"Tough for little boys to lose their mommy."

"It's a wonder they can function at all considering this is the second mother they've lost."

"How can I help you?"

"I need alone time after the funeral. Don't give me that look. I won't desert my boys. I've got to pull myself together."

"I understand, but you're not allowed to sink into a deep dungeon. Your sons won't get better without you."

"Most of me died with Jamie. Our separation makes it even harder. I keep playing 'maybe if' in my brain."

"She would've scheduled lunch with Loretta regardless. She'd have traveled that road."

"I don't know if she stopped loving me. I never told her I loved her and wanted her back home."

"She walked out. It wasn't your doing."

"Maybe if I'd treated Jim better, she'd have stayed with me."

"Don't give the snake any leeway. I'm convinced that his perverted behavior resulted in Jamie's death."

"That makes more sense than someone wanting Jamie dead for something she'd done."

"The boys are welcome to stay with me."

His shoulders hunched, "I know it's a lot of trouble."

"It's not any trouble. They help entertain Sky. Delia is always willing to lend a hand, and I'm sure Opal would assist. You know how she loves your boys—her only grandchildren. If worse comes to worse, I can ask Mom as a last resort. Trust me, it'd be a rare incident if I did."

"After the funeral tomorrow take them home with you. Please tell

Stan thanks for investigating Jamie's case."

"I will. I'll see you at church in the morning. I can't tell you how sorry I am this horrible thing happened to you and your boys. I'm returning to the office to check on clues in Jamie's phone and iPad. I'll return her devices in a few days. Give me a hug and let me leave before I start bawling."

CHAPTER THIRTY-EIGHT

Jamie's family and closest friends gathered in a small room off the sanctuary. They'd fill the front two pews after all the other funeral attendees were seated. Delia and Sloan took Gabriel and Seth to play in one of the Sunday school rooms until time for the family procession.

Lexie's eyes scanned the waiting group: Jim, Opal, Loretta, Adam, Tye, Red, and Margo. Stan stood beside the exit door as requested.

Jim's fists clenched in front of Tye's face. "Why are you here? She didn't give a damn about you. After all those years, she finally realized she married an asshole."

Tye focused on a picture of Jesus that hung on the wall across from him.

Lexie stood in the room's center. "Perhaps this is a bad time to talk about Jamie's murder, but I think she will rest in peace when her killer is locked up."

Loretta's voice tightened, "Who did it?"

Lexie pointed a finger at her, "The clues led me to you."

Margo seethed, "How dare you make such a cruel accusation?"

"The hair found on Jamie's body matches Loretta's DNA."

She squirmed, "I didn't give you DNA."

"You voluntarily gave a sample years ago after three of your basketball team members were murdered."

Her hands gripped each other. "I lied. I didn't stay in the car. I checked Jamie's body. That's why my hair was on her."

Jim's words shot out, "You left her bleeding beside the road?"

His anger hung in the air while Loretta crossed the room and rammed a finger at his chest. "You killed Jamie."

Jim sprang from the folding chair.

Loretta's words poured out, "Jamie said to tell Tye she loved him and was sorry she took your side. Your daughter realized that you're a devil."

"You're full of shit," Jim raved.

Lexie grabbed Loretta's arm and pulled her back. "You said Jamie was dead when you arrived at the site. Now you're quoting her last words? I don't understand."

"Jamie gave me the message for Tye, then died. That's why I was close to her body. I was terrified the killer was still in the woods. I drove home and locked myself in the safe room."

"The coroner said she died almost immediately, "Tye stammered. "Why did you wait so long to contact Lexie?"

"I was petrified."

Lexie's eyes locked on Loretta's face. "Why did you kill your friend?"

Loretta stomped toward the exit then swirled back around to face Lexie. "Don't blame me. It wasn't my fault that I was the one who found her body."

"You lied about posting your luncheon date with Jamie. You were the only one who knew she was driving up your deserted road. You told that Facebook lie to get more suspects in the mix. I committed a law enforcement sin when I didn't verify what you said. That is until last night when I checked your Facebook page on Jamie's iPad and discovered you lied."

Loretta cried out, "I loved Jamie I had no reason to kill her."

Tye's hands shook, "Revenge was your motive."

Loretta lunged toward him. He caught her wrist as she swung a fist toward his face. "You swore you'd never tell about the abortion."

"I didn't tell—you just did."

Lexie's words were calm, even, "Why did you kill Jamie?"

"Jim arranged for the butcher who aborted my baby. My body was ruined forever. My husband left me because I couldn't have babies."

Stan grabbed Jim as he sprang toward Loretta.

Opal's body leaned as her hands grasped her head.

A smirk disfigured Loretta's features. "You son-of-a-bitch, you're the reason Jamie died. You killed my child, and I killed yours. Fair. Even."

The unsuspecting minister stepped into the room to escort the group to the front pews.

"Stan, read Loretta her rights then transport her to jail."

"I'll take care of it, Sheriff."

Loretta fluffed her hair as she winked at Jim. "I'm sure the court will be lenient with me when I turn in a child rapist and a baby killer—you."

CHAPTER THIRTY-NINE

Tye wanted the mourners to leave. They swarmed into his and Jamie's house offering condolences then headed for the fried chicken.

He couldn't eat, and the racket of combined chatter started a relentless throbbing in his head. Everyone talked about plans for tomorrow, or next week, or next vacation. He had no future, only the past.

He made his way through the kitchen chatter and out the back door. One woman asked what he needed. He had to bite his tongue to keep from hollering *my dead wife*. His head gave a negative shake toward the woman and he escaped to the bench under the boy's climbing tree.

Red maneuvered toward him from his own yard escape. "Too much to bear, my friend?"

"Smiles, a little laughter, and lots of noise. It's unbearable."

"Life proceeds regardless of our pain."

Tye pulled a piece of bark from the tree. "That's how it should be. If we cried for other people's troubles, we'd spend all our time wet-faced."

Red sneered, "Here comes that jerk."

"You guys mind if I have a smoke out here?" Stan asked.

"Okay. Thanks for filling in and working with Lexie. I'm in no shape to assist anyone."

Stan looked at Red, "I'd do anything for Lexie."

Red smirked, "She's too good for you."

"That's her decision not yours." Stan dropped ashes at Red's feet. "You deserted her. She deserves a real man—one who'll stay by her side regardless."

"Obviously, you're talking about our breakup because she stole my DNA to solve a case."

Stan blew smoke toward his face. "And you've been whining about it ever since."

"My father died as a result of her fiasco."

"Did you forget it all traced back to Lexie's father—the man your father killed? I don't know why she'd ever forgive you much less love you. Even though you're married she won't move on."

Red spit a wad at his feet. "Are you playing games with her—Mr. Stud?"

"I tried, but I failed because she loves you." Stan moved toward his rental car then walked back. "You're a fool for not asking for her forgiveness."

Tye and Red watched as Stan drove off.

Red kicked the tree. "He's right—my father brought on the trauma, and I placed the blame on Lexie."

"She's still alive, so it's not too late to tell her how you feel."

"I hear you."

Tye vacated the bench. "I'll get back in the house. Maybe folks will take a clue and head home."

"You hope," Red confirmed.

Opal sat alone on the back porch. "Do you have a minute?"

Tye sat beside her and squeezed her hand.

The bags under her eyes were red and swollen. Tears reappeared as she spoke. "I'm so sorry for the burden this has placed on you. I knew Jim was a difficult man, but I didn't know he was evil enough to hurt young girls. I'm leaving him. I'll move back in with my mother in Kansas. She's eighty-five and needs a caregiver, so that'll work out well for her and me both."

"Are you sure that's what you want, Opal?"

"I'm positive. Jim hasn't loved me for years. I love my grandsons, and I don't want to lose contact with them. May I write them? Maybe you'd let them visit me?"

"They love you, and I'll make sure they stay in your life."

She gave Tye a one-armed hug. "A couple of my nephews are here today. They're going to Jim's house with me to pack up my belongings. We'll load my stuff in their truck then we'll head toward my new home."

Tye took the address and phone number she offered. "Be safe," he told her.

The screen door creaked as he entered the house. Jamie had asked him half a dozen times to oil the door. The kitchen was free from gossip now. The chatter was congregated in the living room.

He stood in the archway between the living room and dining room. "Thank you for celebrating Jamie's life. I know she'd be touched by all your love and kindness."

The group stirred from their seats and offered handshakes or hugs as they said good-bye. Within fifteen minutes, the visitors were gone. He heard Lexie and Delia in the kitchen. A glance out the window revealed

Red stacking lawn chairs.

"Boys, let's talk," Seth and Gabriel sat on the coffee table facing him. "Guys, I'm going away for a few days."

Gabriel piped in, "We'll go with you, Daddy."

"I appreciate the offer, but you two have school. I'm so sad I don't want to talk, play ball, or fish. You'll stay with Aunt Lexie and Sky until I get back."

Seth's face threatened tears, "What if you're too sad to come home?"

"I'll be back. It'd make me even sadder not to have my boys. I packed your clothes last night. You can pick out three favorite toys each to take to Aunt Lexie's house. Get it done."

The two scampered away.

Lexie stood in the kitchen doorway. "You told them? Did they take it okay?"

"I think so. I'll phone you every night at seven to check on them. Tell Red I said thanks for helping out today. He's in the yard. I'll pack a few things."

The porch screen closed behind her. "Red?" she hollered.

"I'm here," he called back.

"Tye said thanks."

"Thanks aren't necessary," Red paused as he looked at her face. "Is there something on your mind?"

"I was thinking you, Sky, and the boys could stay at my house. I have lots of room. I admit to an ulterior motive. The hospital said that Hope would be released today. I'd feel less panicked if another adult stayed with us the first few nights."

"I'm glad she's coming home, but I'm unsure about…"

"I bought a baby basket. Hope will stay beside me at night. You can share Sky's room. The boys can sleep in the bedroom on the third floor."

"What time are you picking up Hope?"

"Soon as I've put away these lawn chairs."

"I'll help Delia finish the house cleanup then drop by my place to pack. The three kids and I will likely beat you home."

"That works," he diverted his eyes back to the lawn furniture.

CHAPTER FORTY

Tye's head rested on the disturbed dirt and rock. He laid on his side an arm between the flowers and across the mound that covered Jamie's casket.

"You didn't need to ask for forgiveness; it was always yours. I've loved you since I was seventeen, and I'll love you forever. I'm going away. I'll camp by the lake where we liked to go. Lexie's taking care of Gabriel and Seth. I'll be okay—someday—I think—I hope."

The sun set, the stars appeared, and he continued to caress the mound that covered his wife.

"Tomorrow I'll go to the lake. Tonight I'll stay with you, my love."

EPILOGUE

Seth pushed his math book aside and glanced at the clock that hung on the kitchen wall. "Daddy should've phoned an hour ago."

Lexie looked up from the counter she wiped. "He probably lost track of time."

"This is his fifth day gone, and he's never been even five minutes late to phone us," Seth argued.

"Let's go look for Daddy," Gabriel's worried voice proposed. "What if he's hurt?"

Red maneuvered the bottle nipple into Hope's mouth. "Your dad is a tough guy. I'm sure he's okay. We'll wait a while before we get worried."

"How long is a while, Uncle Red?"

Lexie wasn't sure when the boys started putting *uncle* before Red's name. He didn't seem to mind.

"Couple hours from now. Get your homework finished while Hope drinks her formula. We'll have time to play a game before bedtime."

Sky sat across from Red. She rocked her dolly back and forth holding a small toy bottle in the doll's puckered lips. "Daddy, my baby doesn't suck right."

Lexie smiled. Sky had likely heard those words twenty times from Red's mouth.

"Hope is sucking better tonight. Maybe your baby should watch her."

"Oh, Daddy, my baby can't see. She's pretend."

"That's a good point; however, I thought we pretended she's real."

"Pretend isn't as fun as Hope."

"When it comes to poopy diapers, your doll is more fun."

Sky nodded in agreement then continued the doll's dinner.

A voice yelled from outside the back door. "WHO HAS STOLEN

MY BOYS? I'VE COME TO RESCUE THEM!"

The boys yipped, "Daddy!" in unison.

Lexie swung the door wide. She wasn't positive the man was actually her brother. His clothes were filthy, and a short grubby beard covered his cheeks and chin.

"Come in, stranger, and I mean you look and smell stranger than the last time I saw you."

"A woodsman doesn't require a shave."

Sky held her nose.

Red entered the conversation, "Apparently, he doesn't bathe either."

"I'm smelling ripe—noticed that on my drive home. I'm sure I'll smell better after three or four showers. I stink, but you guys better give me hugs anyway."

Tye sat on a kitchen chair, and the boys each found a knee. Gabriel gave him a sloppy kiss. "You didn't phone on time tonight, Daddy. I was 'worried sick.'"

"Where did you hear 'worried' sick?"

"That's what Nana Delia says."

"You guys pack up your gear; we're headed home."

Sky dropped her dolly and chased the boys up the stairs.

"How are you doing, Bro?"

"Not good, but better. I decided I couldn't survive without my boys close. They're my reason for living."

"They certainly keep a man exercising. I haven't played this much ball since I was twelve," Red said.

"About time you got in shape," Tye joked.

"I'd get up and slug you, but I'm busy rocking my baby."

"What happened with Loretta?"

Lexie handed Tye a bowl of warmed up stew. "Stan transported her to a state women's prison. She claimed temporary insanity and liquor resulted in the death."

A corded neck revealed his anger. "She'd better not get away with Jamie's murder."

"That won't happen. It was premeditated, and she admitted that Jamie's death was revenge against Jim."

"Why was the case sent out of county?"

"I convinced them that it wasn't a good idea to hold Loretta in the county where she killed the sheriff's sister-in-law."

"I'm glad it's out of our jurisdiction. It'd be hard to move forward with the case always in the local paper."

A barrage of noise thundered into the kitchen. "We're ready. Let's go home!" Gabriel demanded.

"Don't you think you should tell Red and Aunt Lexie thank you?"

Seth gave hugs. Gabriel gave kisses, including a soft one on baby Hope's cheek.

"Thank you, Sis. I don't know what I'd do without you."

"Let me get a recorder. I'd like to keep that last statement for eternity."

"No way am I stupid enough to say it twice."

Lexie hugged him, "Call if you need anything."

She helped carry out the boys' belongings. When she returned, she found Sky in the curve of her daddy's right arm with Hope still on the left.

A tear escaped down his cheek. Lexie reached a hand to comfort him. "Hope is okay."

"It's not sadness. This is all I've ever wanted—you, a few kids, and me. The sins of my father took away my dream. Can you ever love me again?"

"I never stopped loving you. Will you forgive me for your father's suicide?"

"I forgave you long ago, but I didn't think you'd ever take me back."

Lexie leaned down and kissed the baby's forehead. "All we needed was a little Hope."

THE END

ACKNOWLEDGMENTS

THANK YOU

To the following individuals, who provided recommendations and professional insights during my writing, editing, and publishing process.

————•————

Teaberry Cover Design, L.K. Campbell, Dan Case, Dana Delamar, Jennette ElNaggar, Kim Woodruff, Daniel Woodruff, Myrna Kurle, Officer Steven Roberts, Kim Roberts, Kayla Grimes, and Detective Brian Gerber.

MORE BY THIS AUTHOR

Sheriff Lexie Wolfe Novels

Killing the Secret
Somebody is murdering the women who played on a championship basketball team twenty years ago. Sheriff Lexie searches for the link between the women that provoked someone to want them all dead.

Deadly Search
Sheriff Lexie becomes entangled in a web of deceit as she searches for her father's murderer. Her temptress mother may be the reason her father was killed.

Terror's Grip
Lexie's right arm suspended above her held by a chain attached to a two-inch metal clamp around her wrist. Her left hand fisted and punched forward as if a boxing bag or her captor's new face dangled in front of her. Her scream filled the cold darkness. "I WON'T DIE WEAK!"

Murder & Beyond
Sheriff Lexie and Deputy Tye Wolfe are enmeshed in the strangest cases of their law enforcement careers. Two teenage girls vanish. Tye doesn't believe that Wendy is a witch. Lexie doesn't think the ocean swallowed Emma.

Deranged Justice
Local citizens panic when Sheriff Lexie doesn't solve a series of bizarre murder cases. An irrationally jealous woman and man who demands custody of her adopted nephew add more turmoil to her life.

NEW RELEASE

Unbreak Their Hearts
Women's Suspense

BEAUTIFUL BAIT
Coming in 2018

JACIE

Jacie woke. Startled, not by the presence of the stranger who slept beside her, but by the stench that escaped through every gland in his body. Her nose tried to avoid the invasion, which resulted in the smell catching in her mouth. The resultant nausea forced her to the bathroom.

Thankfully, the door was shut all night. The smell of mold was a welcome relief. Streaks of urine decorated the faded tan walls in her toilet respite. She sat on the cracked tile. Her eyes followed a curving fissure until it disappeared into the wall. She, too, was looking for a path to follow. Flo, her mom, told her years ago that I-40 went on forever. As of yesterday, Jacie ran away to find out for herself.

Today she sat in a stained motel bathroom, somewhere near a railroad track in Oklahoma City. She longed to scrub the stranger off her smooth skin, and wash him out of her auburn hair. She beckoned him on the highway when her VW bug ran out of gas. Soon after he decided to go to bed—with her under him. She ended up on this cold, cracked floor. Afraid to risk waking up the stranger—no shower for her. She'd wear her stink as armor against any other naked monsters that crossed her path on Interstate 40.

Forcing herself from the floor she returned to the living area. His loud snoring covered her soft escape movements, from the slipping on of her gray jogging pants to the emptying of his wallet.

Jacie grasp his truck key, in her left hand, as she turned the knob and found shelter in an air free of human odor. Fortunately, he parked his orange truck at the far end of the lot. Apparently, he wanted it out of the visual field of car inhabitants driving on Reno Street. She wondered whom he was hiding from: a crazy wife, a jealous girlfriend, or a cop with a warrant. She didn't give a damn *who*, but was glad he hid the vehicle.

The engine started with a roar, as if yelling for help. Her chest tightened. The motel room door didn't stir. No greasy haired monster ran out in a cloud of fumes to chase her down the street.

Three blocks East, Jacie pulled in front of an automotive garage littered with oilcans, and smudges of miscellaneous vehicle liquids. Before she entered, she tied her T-shirt in a knot under her breasts, then pushed her jogging pants to below her belly button.

A gruff voice came from under a disabled car, "What do you want?"

"To borrow a gas can."

"Nothin' around here for loan." Grunts escaped from his massive body as he pushed his roller cart from under the car.

"I'll bring the can right back," she promised.

The man eyed her with appreciation. The gravelly voice turned to smooth stone, "Can't do that."

Blue eyes widened as she pleaded, "Please! I'm dead meat if this truck isn't returned before my friend wakes up."

"Sure don't want a pretty little gal anything but alive. But my trust deserves a reward." The station guy stared at her cleavage.

"What's your pleasure?"

"My ma said I loved breast feeding."

"Five minutes with mine for a gas can loan?"

His oily hand pressed her toward the toilet, "Come with me."

Jacie pulled away. "I'm no fool. You get yours and tell me to get lost." She petted the stubble on the side of his face. "I'll come back. I don't want a big guy like you angry at me."

"Okay, you go pretty one, but I got your license number. If you screw me, you're goin' get screwed."

"I hear you." Jacie lugged the can toward the truck.

She filled the gas can, then found her yellow bug stranded on the highway. The police already marked it for extermination. She parked the truck behind it. Visually scanning the area she saw no sign of stink monster. She slid from the truck seat and retrieved the gas can. Bug drank the liquid and still wasn't full. Jacie threw the can in the back of old orange. Bug and she resumed their journey to the end of I-40.

Jacie's drunken mother and Stinky had more in common than odor. Flo's single twenty, and Stinky's two, left Jacie little cash for survival.

The clouds opened and cleansed the dust off bug as they traveled toward whatever? Jacie didn't think about what was ahead. Such thoughts sharpened the pain in her head. Instead she let her mind dwell on the past as bug left miles behind them.

Flo probably spouted every curse word known to man, when she realized the twenty was gone. The scribbled promise from Jacie that she'd repay her someday was likely stomped on. Flo spit on photos of people who angered her. Jacie imagined a ball of slime rolling down her likeness.

It's too much effort for them to come after me. I'm not worth their time. Stinky will find his rolling orange on the highway. Flo will recite the past, present, and future tenses of the f-word. After a hundred times, she'll say good riddance to her bastard daughter. Gas guy was probably thinking up a lie. Better than trying to explain to his boss the titillating trade. Jacie managed a weak smile.

Her eyes didn't veer from the black asphalt that curved then straightened. Her mind was unclear about the future and darkened from the past.

Days later, if Jacie operated from logic instead of survival she would've asked Zee McCrary what he was up to. She did not ask, because all that mattered was a roof over her head and food in her stomach—*ignorance is innocence* was her new motto.

ZEE

Blood pocketed in the grasp of Zee's right hand as he climbed the six-foot ladder to the hunter's perch. His dark eyes searched the wooded area for Goliath. He heard leaves crumble as the lion came toward him. Goliath crept forward in pursuit of his prey. His ribs tensed as he spied the squirrel that Zee extended above the enclosure.

Zee lifted the small animal with one leg nailed to the pole's end. He made a swinging arch above the big cat's head and swung back and forth.

The animal bared his teeth, then a suffering growl raged out.

Zee mimicked, shouting back a hoarse groan and clicking his yellowed dentures. Soon bored, Zee lowered the pole and watched the lion rip the squirrel apart. The crunch of bone and flesh only lasted seconds. The lion's body moved back and forth as he stalked his owner.

"You're thinking my flesh and bones will make a good supper after your squirrel appetizer. It ain't happening, but good news. I hired a beautiful girl to bring men into our trap. Food for you, sport for me, and society gets rid of bottom suckers." Zee licked the squirrel blood from his fingers as he walked toward the barn.